Memento Mori

JACK KELLY

ISBN-13: 978-0-9909944-8-0

E-Book ISBN-13: 978-0-9909944-9-7

DEDICATION

For the City

ACKNOWLEDGMENTS

Thanks for the Internet, Google Search and Wikipedia for assists large and small.

PART I: No Rest for the Wicked

May you be in heaven a full half hour before the devil knows
you're dead.

- A Traditional Irish Toast

The Devil's Dues

A tall thin form enters into the room unnoticed and unchallenged. He'd passed through the entire building this way and to this point. It's not a surprise really, just a simple matter of claiming one's property. He steps about the room with a familiarity which perhaps should come as no surprise to anyone who has been paying any attention so far.

He walks over to the row of coolers and selects the drawer with the corpse he wants. He pulls open the drawer and then removes his hat and holds it in his right hand against his chest as he slouches a bit to get a closer look at Jackie Boy. He cocks his head a degree left and right seeming to decide on something before he stands up straight and takes in a very deep breath the kind one does when they know how the immediate task before them will be a little difficult and possibly unpleasant or perhaps in the opposite order and which one might wish to steel themselves for it gather up amass a little fortitude for the coming ordeal.

The tall thin man sets his hat to the side on the tray with the coroner's tools and then leans in over Jackie Boy again and taps a long finger on his chest before sitting up straight next to Jackie Boy or what's left of him at any rate. He pulls a case from somewhere and gets to work humming some strange haunting tune.

The tall thin man leans over Jackie Boy absently chewing on a large cut of something like its chewing tobacco except this appears to be of a tougher material judging by the way he works his jaws. He seems to be inspecting his past handiwork and the x shaped scar he'd left in Jackie Boy's chest from their previous encounters probing it with his fingers and raising the memory of the pain to the surface.

The tall thin man pulls the same plain evil looking black lick of flame knife which had previously carved a very straight line over Jackie's heart and holds it over those same wounds scarred over know but seeming to cry out in greeting eager for the ancient blade to commit to its work anew. The tall thin man closes his eyes as both hands wrap around each other and the hilt of the blade hovering like a divining rod or some other such weird hoodoo shit as he seems to fall into a meditative trance offering up a long prayer over the scene.

The man's fingers traced the scar as the ancient knife descends to re-slice the same very straight line on Jackie's chest. The thin man continues on with his work as he sets the wicked looking knife to the side for the moment before placing his hands on either side of the wound to open it further with a good hard pull of his hands in opposite directions to shoot a new bolt of pain throughout his body, near blinding pain too. The thin man's sharply pointed fingernails work their way into his body til he grasps something within Jackie utters a Huh and then retracts his hand which is no less painful for the removal.

The thin man raises his hand to his mouth where his teeth and gums are working at something seemingly stuck between his teeth and trying to work it out his hand reaches up to his mouth to extract what he'd been chewing on pulling out a dark purple red hunk of gore, blood and tissue revolting Jackie Boy with the sight of the mass which he strangely recognizes as his own flesh and blood.

The thin man places the chunk into Jackie Boy's chest his own personal missing piece of heart working his sharpened fingers in Jackie Boy's chest doing who knows what before through an extremely agonizing moment before removing his hand to take up the knife again against his own thumb producing a small slice before running the bleeding digit through Jackie's wound and then raises them up to his lips to lick clean.

The thin man pats the carving smoothing it with his own blood to reseal the wound and placing his hand on Jackie's chest as he chants what can only be an incantation or prayer to an ancient and terrible blood god of some sort or another. This is a false imagining as Ol' Jackie Boy cannot really see the tall thin man on his knees to any other kind of a deity or whatever higher power he currently called upon.

The tall thin man lifts him to a sitting position and restarts him with a thump on his back. Thump not entirely describing it or giving it its proper representation in reality. It was more like a decidedly hard whack more than a love tap but what did you expect then after all. A cough a hacking cough like he swallowed something he shouldn't have and the tall thin man as nursemaid as disturbing as this visual is coaxing him to life, to breathe until he achieves it on his own brining a thin grin to the thin man's face who then lays him back down on the pavement. Wipes the sweat from his brow coughing a small but himself and Jackie Boy thinks how odd this is, how strange indeed.

The tall thin man has put back Jackie Boy's missing piece now but only part enough to give life or something like it back to him and some people might mistake this description for sounding very zombie like and they are forgiven for drawing such an erroneous conclusion as we've been alluding this way. This is something else entirely some dark art known to otherworldly creatures who shun the light, this grants the tall thin man not control exactly so much as an ability to point in a direction and perhaps ask a favor of one so afflicted and which person simply might have to do the deed as it were without raising much of a complaint, a useful little thing as everyone knows the devil prefers to not actually get his own hands dirty if he can help it which is why he likes humans so much for their pliability.

The tall thin man, for reasons all his own, had decided there was a need for the continuation of the trek undertaken by our hero Ol' Jackie Boy. To what purpose was not entirely clear past the tall thin man's own statement of how Ol' Jackie was too amusing to kill.

"Dead man," the thin man says to him, "it's time now dead man, time to get to it."

The thin man leans in to Jackie's raised form then and provides him with a list of particulars for him to act on as he sees fit and all in good time if you will. No reason is given for the list of particulars, though some most align with goals which our intrepid hero Ol' Jackie Boy might find himself amendable to anyway.

Jackie finds himself warming up to the idea which pleases the thin man who smiles at the progress made. He likes this man for the near pure chaos he causes as he blissfully plunges forth in misguided aspirations which serve to feed the thin man. He was an ancient creature who thrived on chaos in any form and this man here was one of the more creative and inventive forms off it and completely oblivious to it which he'd ever encountered in all his years stuck wandering this rock.

Our Hero Ol' Jackie Boy finds himself nodding his head in agreement to the many points being made by the thin man. He's finding the argument presented to be rather persuasive and feel amendable to acting upon it accordingly. This seems to please the thin man who allows what passes for a smile over his face to occur. It is one of the worst sights our hero Ol' Jackie Boy has ever seen. The thin man is pleased with the results of a good night's work and leaves Ol' Jackie Boy with one of those patented shiver up and down ones spine laughs from the man as he walks out into the embrace of the night air.

Dead Man's Blues

The morgue's the same as any other morgue might looking much like one might expect which is to say not at all like the ones on TV. There's only bright lighting featured over the tables where the work is done. Serious work by serious minded people long inured to the knowledge of looking at lifeless bodies. Whether they ponder the mysteries of the struggle of life and death is never discussed but seems doubtful once you've been given a glimpse into the inner workings of these things and find there isn't much mystery to be discovered there.

Jackie Boy's simply minding his own business as he lies in the drawer freshly scrubbed nude and unmindful of the cold. He's feeling appreciative of the fresh scrub too, had been feeling how he was well past time for a bath after all. He felt fresh and pinkish and not dwelling too hard over the fact of any sense of feeling or why he should be feeling anything at all after all considering he was dead and all.

It's a good way to go or to be presented, at any rate, for whatever comes next, especially if it's going to be judged as had been reported. One thing Ol' Jackie Boy remembers from a lifetime of shit is to always look presentable when going to court and before the judge like it somehow excuses all the dirt you tracked in regardless of your off the rack new blue suit.

The room, the instruments used and the hands of the coroner or more probably one of his flunkies and toe tag hanging are aligned and prepared and waiting as they haven't cut him open yet. Somehow it's doubtful there'll actually be an autopsy asked for or performed, not with this many gunshot wounds present. It makes for a fairly easy matter of determining the whole cause of death thing, you know, lead poisoning.

Well fuck this is disappointing Jackie Boy is thinking about the situation. No light to go into, no one of any kind loved or not to greet one on the other side or to make the trip easier and less fearful like told on all those stories. No other side at all, just this darkness. No heaven or hell and nothing else either apparently, just cold and darkness absolute in both regards. He realizes as he's slid out he's lying in what turns out to be a metal sliding drawer toes first and the first face he sees is the tall thin man and his wicked black flame knife standing over him leaving him somehow not surprised at the development.

Jackie Boy's thinking this is the promised replay of a moment from his life like has been described as a plausible review watch person gets upon their death and shortly before where ever it is they're fated for. Jackie watches the replay fascinated as the thin man he'd called or thought of as the tall thin man. He dispassionately watches as the thin man works with his hands and his knife at Jackie Boy's chest humming to himself or reciting a prayer or an invocation of some sort bringing the air around Jackie Boy to a vibrating hum in rhythm with the tall thin man and reaches a certain pitch when the thin man takes his wicked looking black knife and flicks it out across his chest and then into it across the neat hard slice it had carved there before.

Excruciating pain shoots through Jackie Boy made doubly more so from the remembrance of the first time the wound had found its way into Jackie's chest. Never mind how he should be beyond pain considering he's dead and all. He hears the thin man laugh and knows this is something else entirely. The thin man's laugh is not from something human but from something old and ancient despite the form the thin man chose for his walking about.

"Come now dead man," the thin man says, "time's a wasting, time to get to it," or this is what our intrepid hero Ol' Jackie Boy thinks he heard said before he passes back into the darkness.

Jackie Boy wakes in the darkness thinking he's just had a very vivid bad dream for reasons unclear other than a memory with a hole through it. He feels generally awful near every part of his body, a general ache through every part of him. He tries to move but finds himself confined except for a slight sliver of light on three sides above his head. He manages to move his arms upward to find purchase there to pull himself up, but instead he pulls himself out.

He hears the sliding of steel wheels in steel grooves as he slides out into the subdued light of a room unfamiliar. He looks about at the institutional tile in soothing colors and realizes he's in the city morgue during it's off hours, as if there is such a thing. He's caught now in a strange place of confliction, and doesn't rightly know whether to be relieved pleased or mad as hell.

The morgue isn't the issue for him as it was where he'd been heading anyway, so, no surprise there, no. The surprise is to be in the morgue and still in and of this world by whatever means the thin man had used. This is the worst part of a nightmare, the lack of finality and a return to the world which had never delivered anything but bitter pain and disappointment to him and everything he'd touched.

The thin man had said something about it though, how things were left undone without getting into anything more specific, which might seem a mistake unless one's open to the idea he'd done it on purpose knowing how a lack of specifics is our intrepid hero Ol' Jackie Boy's personal bailiwick, the grey area arena where he was most comfortable in. Back from the dead courtesy of the thin man adding a whole new meaning to the phrase working for the man, an irony perhaps amusing from an outside looking in perspective exclusively mind you, not so amusing on the other side of the screen.

The Mistress

Jackie Boy leaves the morgue feeling like death warmed over and not appreciating the context of the phrase even if it has never previously been more appropriately used. He exits through the loading dock and briefly thinks of stealing an ambulance except it feels a little obvious. He instead opts to walk back to the Quarter as he feels how he's got time to kill as he attempts to sort through and absorb a host of thoughts and realities which strike from the pages of fictions more than they do any reference for things which should actually be.

He does a quick check of his pockets and finds a couple of crumpled bills and some loose change tangled amidst the lint and other detritus of his pockets. It's enough for a tall boy and this being New Orleans he doesn't have far to go in either time or distance to find a corner store open.

There's a thin old man getting the stove in back ready for the morning rush and a large woman behind the cash register. Neither pays him any mind as he reaches into the cooler in front of the register and comes out with his tall boy and places it on the counter. The woman rings it up on the old fashioned cash register, possibly the oldest of the trio behind the counter, taking his crumpled bills and making change before returning back to her taciturn watch.

Jackie Boy grabs a brown paper bag from off the top of the counter and slips his tall boy into it, cracking the tab on top and taking a good long swallow of the cold gold beverage which he's always found to be satisfying. He takes another drink as he steps out and turns in the street to head towards the Quarter once more in no particular hurry. Jackie knows that he's killing time, telling himself he was thinking things over, even debating his destination as if he really had any other place to go.

He's uncertain of the reception he'd receive if he should darken her doorway once more, he doesn't know how much time has passed or hasn't no watch or calendar to tell him either. He doesn't know what she'd heard or possible seen with her abilities and knew about the gun battle and its reported results. Wasn't certain if it'd be a shock or not should he turn up on her doorstep as he seemed to do with some form of regularity which he could not explain. Always ending up down at her place welcome or not.

He was still debating things even as his feet guided him in the familiar path deep into parts of the Quarter where only those who live here in this crescent city have cause to be in or know of it. The streets are quiet once past Bourbon Street the din behind him as he crosses St Phillip to turn down Ursulines at the next corner to find his stop.

His tall boy is long gone as he stands across the street from her place. He knows why he's hesitant as he remembers how things had been left between the two of them the last time he'd occupied her sofa. It was goodbye forever she'd said when he'd walked out into the night. He'd thought she 'd said it because she was mad, a hurtful statement thrown out after a person has already stepped out on the course of action which had caused the argument in the first place.

He realized now how it hadn't been anything from anger at all. It had been a predictor of the future, a consequence she could see from the decision he'd made, from the choice to do more of his hero shit. A choice made in spite of all the ample warnings leading up to the confrontation Jackie Boy had sought out. The Mistress herself on more than one occasion telling him the same thing if only he'd heeded her but clearly hadn't out of stubbornness or obtuseness hardly the point.

There was no ill will which he bore her should he arrive at her door and find there was no sympathy to be had there. It wouldn't surprise him at all to find his welcome a little worn out at this point in time, a decided lack of happy to see you. All of it deserved mind you, well-earned and an a rare example of The Mistress exercising some of her good common sense in regards to our hero Ol' Jackie Boy for a change.

Bad penny she'd called him on more than one occasion as he continued to run up his debt with her over the years despite his inability to ever even it out. She must have known it and still she has allowed him to pass into her inner sanctum without too many questions put to him. Then there was the way they'd left it the last time they'd occupied the same space was a source of potential uncertainty and uneasiness lying there between them. He didn't know if he had the strength to face an uncertain reception which awaited him should he darken her doorway once more especially after the night he'd already had.

He's standing outside her door, technically still the street as he stares at the door of the home of the woman he calls the Mistress. He steps up to the door of the house which Lulu, The Mistress, calls home and where he usually winds up and still he hesitates, wanting another tall boy to ease his mind. Finally he raises his hand and knocks at her door lightly like he's afraid to be heard and trying only the slightest effort while secretly hoping to not get an answer.

There's a delay which is steadily turning into a longer delay and he's right about to give up when the door opens a sliver and an eye peers out for another long moment, long enough to make him shift his weight from foot to foot and clears his throat while he waits counting down the seconds like they're minutes and weighted heavily as well so they might pass with a thud. He's trying to decide how much longer he waits until he gives it up for good and turns to leave when he hears a voice from behind him telling him to stop and turn round.

He obeys the voice, turning round to see the door is open and she's standing there in a gossamer gown looking him up and down for more very long moments like she's determining exactly what it is she sees before her. For a change Ol' Jackie Boy wisely and unusually doesn't say a single damn thing and this is by far the smartest tack he could have taken. A half smile appears at the corners of her mouth and soon flickers away as her eyes rise up to his face and she raises her arm to the block the other half of the doorway and introduce her hip into the space in a clear indication of not welcome here.

"Come round again have you now," she says leaving the question to hang in the space between the two of them a moment of uncomfortable silence the air all about them or at least about him as he stands in the street holding absolutely still making him very mindful of the heat and sticky humidity as the phrase hangs there as he's at a loss for something to say or do in answer to her.

"Suppose it was inevitable I'd find you here to darken my doorway once more I guess," she adds after another moment but still she has not moved nor given any indication she will do anything more than stand in the doorway leaving him in the street.

"Damn you bad penny," she says more under her breath then out loud, her right hand is still up high on the doorway and the other is on the knob of the door behind her hip as she leans against the door. She's debating what her decision should be, unhappy with the few options she can see in this regard. She knows she's going to regret it either way she decides and seems to be looking for the lesser of the two when there aint no damnded difference in the matter at hand.

She audibly sighs and takes a step back into her house a scowl on her face evidenced by the curl of her lip in its right corner, beautiful lips carrying the shock of the red against her naturally pale complexion and all of the black she typically wore as she stepped inside her home. He swears for a moment he hears her mutter, 'must be out of my damned mind,' shaking her head at yet another foolish decision but then she always did have a soft spot for Jackie Boy. This being another point as she leaves her door way unguarded, however temporarily, but long enough for Ol' Jackie Boy to dart inside before it can close and shut him out even though what he faces inside is far from certain too.

He scuttles inside trying hard not to focus in the less than flattering imagery the word conjures up. He settles himself inti her couch and waits for whatever it is which comes next as he can hear her rummaging in her kitchen from somewhere behind him. She emerges a short while later with two Miller High Life's unopened in her hands. She hands them both to him and he dutifully cracks the pair open keeping one for himself and returning one to her to her still standing form looking like she's thinking hard about her decision and weighing both the consequences of it and of the avenues forward in regards to it as well.

"Dare I ask you just here in the hell you've been all this time," she says as she raises her own High Life to her lips painted a dark red in match to the color dark red painted on her fingertips as well. Perhaps one is a different shade or hue from the other and yet the colors are perfect and unbroken on her lips and nails equally. He watches and envies the path of the cold beer as he sees it trace a path along the beautiful line on her throat, his imagination briefly running wild and inappropriately. She stops for a moment and he swears she knows his thoughts and he becomes self-conscious about those strays.

Jackie Boy has no answer for her mostly because he doesn't rightly know where he's been other than the obviousness of the morgue. But how to explain a story which starts with him being dead in the morgue and then every impossible thing stretching from there to here in a preposterous chain of implausible events even for someone like himself with his famous continuous streak of bad luck.

She stays standing at the corner of the couch examining him with a critical eye which either is silently adding up all of his aches or simply his tab. It was of no mind really whichever way it was she was tabulating as neither was a balance sheet he wanted to see heavily tilted to the one side of what's owed anyway. He takes a pull off of the slim bottle of High Life trying not to think of the irony applicable in the beverage's name as he waits on her to decide whichever way she's going to go about this deciding he has nothing to say, possibly the single smartest choice he could make in the here and now.

Her High Life is already empty but has done nothing to douse her anger which gives her hips a nice roll to them underneath her black dress as she moves to disappear deeper into the houses' interior, into places which he's not allowed to know or see private chambers and more. The secrets of a woman Jackie Boy thinks actually drawing a brief and crooked smile across his cragged face which he's glad The Mistress isn't there to witness or there'd be hell to pay.

The Mistress was most certainly a woman with secrets, with many secrets and mysteries about her beginning with her given name of Lulu which Jackie was rarely granted the privilege of using and is unused to uttering. Lulu was a name which could be defined as someone wonderful or remarkable which she certainly was, and thus an apt description for her. Back some years, the English would have called her witch and noted the misappropriation of the name meaning light and probably of burned her for it.

In the Teutonic languages and others as well, it meant famous in battle and it was this description which Jackie Boy preferred the best for her though he always kept this under careful wraps, it wouldn't due for the Mistress to know all which he'd found out one rainy day when stuck in the library mostly for its lack of rain. This is what happens when you get terribly bored and a startling spark of curiosity drives you to suddenly need to know whatever you can about a subject leading him to all of the above information now carefully guarded against the displeasure of the one person whom still had a soft spot for him, a spot which he couldn't dare risk.

Though he himself is surprised he could recall it even if he couldn't recall what, other than rain and time to kill, had drove him to read up on it. His mind is brought back from it wanderings when she returns to the couch to sit next to him a white bowl in front of her with her mending supplies within it. Without preamble or warning she begins to examine Jackie Boy for any wounds he has this time, sue to be surprised when there are none which she can discover.

"In it again huh Jackie," she says after a moment having given up her search for any injuries uncertain whether to be surprised at his apparent lack of any and the reason behind them though she had her suspicions in this regard. Jackie simply shrugs his shoulders in answer to her in indifference to it. Acknowledging the situation for what it is and, not wanting to push his luck with her, resisting the temptation to raise his hands in the classic what are you going to do gesture.

"You don't have to tell me Jackie," she says, "it's fairly plain you're in it up to your head again."

He still finds he has nothing to say to her and takes a sudden and very deep interest in the level of beer left in his thin clear bottle of High Life wishing for a second and more while knowing it was presumptuous of him to think there was more of this in his near future or before he'd wear out his welcome he before then.

The Mistress doesn't look disappointed, just tired. She'd known better than to expect an answer. Or, and perhaps more accurately, she'd already known what the answer would be which she shortly confirms.

"Already past the point aren't you Jackie," she asks him with something like anger and defeat in her tone when she does. She looks at him as he refuses to look her way which brings a frown to her face as she puts her drink down for moment and mumbles should have known to herself as she's shaking her head in disbelief and then says to him.

"So," she begins, "tell me then, what is your sorry foolish notion for this particular go-round of yours this time?"

Jackie's still at a loss though, still has no answer to provide her still without a place to start or a plausibility to secure a story to. He thinks about telling her of his encounter with the thin man and his offer to avenge but she'd already called him on his penchant for what she called the 'hero shit' of his and would have cause to seriously wonder if he hadn't learned anything from the first time round. It leaves him with no words forthcoming though and his mouth as it hangs open followed by a shrug of his shoulders.

"There's nothing I can tell you which you'd believe," he finally says to her. She looks at him in straight disbelief considering all the pair has been through up to and including his literal dead ass being here presently on her couch. She is now the one at a loss for an answer as she's staring incredulously at Ol' Jackie Boy sitting on her couch, in her house, the bad penny returned as he always seems to do and with a story *he* claims *she* won't believe. It's almost too much.

She begins to laugh at his comment, a little girl kind of giggle too which's a little strange to hear from a grown adult woman especially the Mistress. It's not something he would have expected from the way she usually comported herself and it is this incongruity which breaks the impasse. She turns her head to look away from him to catch her breath and to gather herself and prepare as best she can for whatever story he has for her which could fit within the category of not to be believed which exists in a thin space between the two of them and seemingly narrowing all the time. Her curiosity is piqued though and she wants to rise to the challenge laid down by Jackie Boy's pretense.

"Oh," she says as she turns back to Ol' Jackie Boy with an eyebrow raised, tucking her feet underneath her on the couch as she faces him, "try me Jackie."

Jackie Boy looks at her trying to read her intentions but she's giving no indication one way or the other as to which way she's leaning towards. Skepticism or openness as her reception of whatever he has to say. He hesitates unwilling just yet to begin, still stuck there with where to start and he decides to just highlight it for her.

He gives her the brief story without interruption and finishes by raising and draining his High Life. He waits a moment as she digests the information and she nods her head like it's not such the strange story told, or the strangest thing she's heard with Jackie Boy wondering if this was due to her ability to see past this particular existence, if it's her own reasoning or if it's once again something she's seen. She's quiet for a bit, he doesn't quite know how long nor or be able to later recall, before she uncoils from the couch in a sudden and near violent upward trajectory propelled by her anger.

"Dammit Jackie!" She says, "How many times do I have to tell you how this hero shit aint for you!"

She stands at the end of the couch her anger radiating off of her hot and roiling towards our hero Ol' Jackie Boy. It seems ready to pour forth in a long stream of rhetoric in a furtherance of the no hero argument but none is forthcoming as she stops literally in her tracks as the expression goes, and the first time he's physically witnessed such a thing.

She's realizing something which has been there all the time in front of her and easy to see, sight or not, but finally revealed by her anger. There was no sense in trying to argue Jackie Boy out of the hero bend he was on. No matter the volume used, it wasn't going to have any more effect this time than it had all the other times attempted. It had to difficult an obstacle to overcome which it had little chance versus his hard headedness. A hard headed sonnaofabitch who is seemingly determined to stay on a set course of action and the thought she'd realized which had made her stop dead in her tracks.

"This here hero shit is going to kill you for sure this time Jackie," she sighs seeming genuinely upset over the notion which is the more disconcerting thing to him past her dire warnings. Not sure if it's an easy prediction because she saw it or because it's an easy thing to see especially the way he goes about things, his penchant for this behavior despite all notions against the very idea of it. This is the very thing she's realized and which had given her pause in her diatribe as calm descends over her.

"I think you know it too Jackie," she pronounces her realization out loud, "I think you know it and have for a while now which is why you've been doing your damndest to catch up to it because you want to."

She finishes her revelation and turns away from him one hand on her hip the other raised to her chin in the classic pose of contemplation. She takes a step away and then back more or less pacing in place in search of something, a decision she feels has to be reached, no, correction, is already reached it just needs to be said and only two things keep it from being unvoiced for both a lack of words and concern for how it will be received with more emphasis in the former than the latter.

"I shouldn't be surprised," she says still having most of this portion of the conversation with herself, "you've been heading straight for it Jackie and you're about to get what you've been asking after all his time."

She stops here again looking back at Jackie Boy sitting on the couch almost looking forlorn except, and she reminds herself this, he is the cause of his own impending demise. One cannot continue to go out looking for trouble and not expect it to pay some form of dividend or otherwise in reward for the constant flirtations and the dogged pursuit thereof.

"I won't be a party to it Jackie," she say freeing the words of the decision she'd reached, "I don't want to be anywhere near it when the crashing comes Jackie. So go and do you're hero shit Jackie and when it kills you kill you off for good just do me a favor and keep stepping off into the next forever and don't bother to come round my door anymore, you're no longer welcome here."

Finished with what she had to say she smooths her hands down the length of the front of her dress as she looks left and right about the room one leas time like she's trying to memorize the details of the place in this moment. It's a strange thing to witness her doing in her own home, a place she navigates easily knowing every square inch of the place. She turns a half step in profile to him now her long black hair cascading down to cover her face and her expression which Jackie feels strangely thankful for.

"I expect you to be gone when I come back to this room," she says and walks out from the main room of the house. Her anger undiminished giving her hips a nice roll to them underneath her black dress as she moves to the dark parts unknown deep in the back of her house where Jackie Boy has never had license or permission to even wonder about let alone dare visit.

Jackie Boy briefly thinks to say something to The Mistress' back as she disappears but knows there's no protest to offer in return to her statement. She'd been both fairly clear and accurate and he doesn't begrudge her any of them or thee decision reached. In a strange turn he's a little surprised it took this long for her to throw him out to his own devices, as it felt like it was well past time now for him to go and face the world once more.

Jackie Boy sits up straight from his place on the couch and stands placing the empty High Life bottle on the side table there. He takes a moment to straighten up his clothes before he goes to her door to step out into the waiting arms of the night.

He leaves her house without so much as a look back, for whatever Jackie Boy is and is not he has never been the type of person to look backwards. He is a straight ahead kind and not a sentimental type and still he feels what to most would be seen as an ominous chill as her house disappears at his back as he walks away.

The ominous chill of how she'll never put her eyes upon him again, ever cast a look in his direction and not out of spite or pity or any other such narrative notion how her eyes will never find him again. It's a simple matter similar to the reason she had revoked his right to appear on her doorway, bad penny or not. It was a matter of too painful to look at him when one can look at him and see his future so clearly like The Mistress could and apparently had here when the devil comes calling to claim what's rightfully owed and was already owed and would soon come to be collected. The devil after all was in the details of these things and now, we learn, in the timing of things as well in streak of famously bad luck.

Jackie steps into the Quarter trying to determine if this row with the Mistress is a part of his bad luck streak or a result of it like there's a difference which could be found or parsed out and like the balance hung in the answer. He steps straight ahead on a path undetermined as his thoughts turn to the promise of vengeance which the thin man had vaguely hinted at and the first step he could take in this direction and screw the fine print details of the decision made. Jackie the poster

Boy for nothing left to loose and not knowing the untruth of the statement.

The Lost Girl

He walks away from the Mistress' door without destination or direction to turn into. It's a curious time of say to be out and about with the late night turning to early morning which leaves the streets of the Quarter mostly empty save serious night owls, lost drunks, and the garbage collectors and street cleaners prepping for the start of another day.

He's been wandering about the Quarter he doesn't know how long as it's easy to loose time in the Quarter. He wanders because he lacks somewhere to go, he tell himself if he'd go somewhere if he had a place in mind which would take him. His old place was most likely long gone, and he'd clearly worn out his welcome at the Mistress' house. He'd had thoughts of taking solace in the nearest bar until he reached into this pocket and rediscovered his lack of funds there where a loose key unremembered tumbles around his fingers.

He raises the discovered the key up and remembers it's the key to Sissy's old place a place which he hadn't been back to since gravity had come to claim her. He stares at the key like it has an answer it can provide him, some clue but all it can do is open a door to a place, an empty space which is as good a place as any to lie low, grab a shower and then some rest, to hideaway from the world for a day or two as he tried to sort through or make sense of all which has transpired in a very short amount of time.

Sissy's place is actually not too far from the Mistress house a short jaunt up towards Rampart and over a short distance and he'd be there if he remembers it right. Sissy had herself nice quiet little house down past Dumaine on Burgundy in a quiet part of the Quarter. Jackie reaches her house and steps up to its door hoping the key still fits the lock sending along a wish and a hope so with the twist of the key til he hears a satisfying click of tumblers and the crack of the door as it releases from the hold the jamb had on it.

Inside the air of her quaint, small, and comfortable if unoccupied house, the air is still, warm and stale, smelling of dust and of being enclosed. He wonders if some of her things are sure to still be here to be found and remind him, physical things to tie into memories and ghosts to haunt him as he enters the house. The house looks untouched from what he remembers of it but right now he doesn't take the time to reflect on the comparison.

He's exhausted as he climbs the stairs to the second floor following the way to her room from imprinted memory without the bother of having to think about where he's going. He peels out of his clothes and lets them fall to the floor as he clicks on the overhead fan before lying down on her bead on his back to stare at the ceiling. He's trying hard not to think of her as he lies in her space in the bed which is possibly not the best way to accomplish this goal of his leaving him lying there trying to settle his mind thinking sleep isn't ever coming up to claim him.

Jackie Boy slips into the murky space between awake and asleep with no indication to its boundaries. It's a dangerous no-man's land where the line between worlds blurs and becomes indistinct and upon waking is rendered into something which can never be accurately recalled. Jackie is wandering these depths as his body back in her bed reaches out for her and finds nothing but empty space and remorse from which Jackie Boy mumbles out her name, Sissy.

"I'm a ghost Jackie," comes a voice from the murky space, "now why won't you let me be?"

"Sissy," he says again though more like a question this time as he rolls restless and too hot under the single sheet on the bed where he is joined by a petite form. Her nude body fits in along his right side under his arm which comes to alit along her side his fingertips resting lightly on her hip. His whole body relaxes and a sigh escapes as he descends deeper into sleep

"I'm right here Jackie," she says her voice sounding more subdued than he recalls it ever being before.

"You seem sad," he notes, "don't be sad."

"Jackie," she says, "I'm dead and gone now why won't you let me go, why are you holding on to me?"

"My fault Sissy," he mumbles and she sighs and seems sadder than she had only a moment before.

"You need to stop this hero shit Jackie," she says, "I need it even less now I'm on the other side. So please stop before too it's too late."

Jackie falls into a silence then as he squeezes her closet to him. She sighs because she knows her words have been futile and landed on too hard headed a target. It's clear to her in a way things can only be to those who are dead and gone he's not going to give up the hero shit just as he's unwilling to let her go too, and if he won't then, she'll have to be the one to make the break then.

She moves under the covers until she's in tip of him a trail of her small kisses from his shoulder to his mouth. They make bittersweet love in the moonlight and then, of course, she's gone with the dawn even as Jackie Boy is waking and reaching for her thinking she's still there but he's alone of course except for the memories and a heavy sadness hanging on his chest making it hard to breath despite it's not being real.

Jackie Boy's left with nothing but the memory of the girl, of his searching the spot on the bed next to him for her held in some form of a sainted memory of her unasked for and unwanted as evidenced by her visit. A ghost she had told him last night in the dream and now in the waking hours she is still every bit of dead and gone. His limbs are stiff and uncooperative as he attempts to rise and shake off the visitation from the night before. He doesn't rightly know if this is the correct word for what to call it and supposes this might pass as the price to be paid for living with ghosts and for as a long as he chooses to stay in Sissy's apartment.

She like a dream or a nightmare or a product of his extreme tiredness mixed with mourning and guilt on top of the stresses he had experiences over the past half day since he'd walked out of the morgue.

He doesn't want to dwell on it too long as it gives him a pounding headache which he felt he hadn't drank enough to deserve.

Jackie Boy's managed to shift to sitting up with his feet on the floor and his head in his hands hunched over on the edge of the bed with the memory of the lost girl still clinging to him and lingering. He can fell the absence of her, the loss of her though there's no way which the word loss can adequately describe what he's feeling. Missing her too does the feeling a disservice for what Jackie Boy knows is a forever ache, for something which he'll carry with him and possibly forever. If he were a different sort he might shed a tear over it.

But our hero Ol' Jackie Boy here hasn't cried in years, doesn't rightly know how or the why of it. Yes he's missing her now, but there's nothing which can be done about it. There is however something which can be done to perhaps even out the scales just like the thin man had told him. Take down a man called King to bring balance back to the scales for the girl lost, to even things out in the universe. The lost girl's innocence versus the man called King and his proclivities. It was an idea which Jackie Boy liked very much and thought it was well past time to get to it. He rises from the bed and heads for the shower to get a fresh head of stream on the task ahead of him.

The One Armed King

The man called King sits behind his ruined desk in the middle of his shot to hell office. He is wearing a wide collared gold colored shirt opened at the neck and missing its customary tie or, correction the tie is being used as an impromptu sling to hold his now useless left arm in tight against his torso lest it hang lifeless at his side where it had been left after a smash of a bullet or two from the would be hero responsible for all of this destruction in the very seat of his empire.

The one armed King sits behind his desk thinking of what his off the books doctor had told him when he'd arrived and before he'd told him the arm was going to be permanently inert except for a promise of to remind him of what it had once been before. The doc had said he was a lucky man, lucky to be alive but he doesn't feel lucky at all. No, he certainly didn't feel lucky between his arm and bandages still over his left eye and ear with wounds which are destined to turn into scars, or so the doc had told him before finishing the first aid. King's once handsome face to now bear a curl upon his chin and cheek stopping any growth of beard from ever forming there.

Upon King's desk rests a nickel plated pistol, his own personal piece pulled out from a bank safety deposit box just for the occasion of the want to be hero called Jackie Boy. This Jackie Boy being the dumb sonnaofabitch who'd been the reason behind all of King's troubles of late and all over a girl, over a piece of ass on the periphery of King's empire.

King's still surprised over the amount and lengths of trouble this one man fuck up had caused over a little girl. He has heavy duty pain pills lined up in front of him like good little soldiers and is casually popping them intermixed with whiskey as he counted the costs this one man walking disaster had caused him. It started obviously with King himself shot and ran the gamut all the way to Joey Bones dead and gone.

Most disturbing to King though is the absence of a confirmation of the would be hero as deceased. King felt certain the hero should be dead, swears he'd seen the bullets riddle the stupid motherfucker himself before he himself had gone down with multiple gunshots received of his own.

King had sent his new consigliere, who is no Joey Bones by a long , to find out and a disturbing report had come back to him of how there was no body in the morgue. King was incredulous but didn't have much time to think about this improbability when last he recalls he had sworn he had seen the man go down under a hail as it was said in crime novels. But no death is official until there's a body found, it was an old rule learned by King many years ago long before he was known as King and just a simple street soldier.

Find him then King says through gritted teeth opening a bottle of whiskey to accompany the lined up pain pills as his new man departs with soldiers in tow to assist him. King raised the glass to his lips and took a good long swallow and then poured out another glassful as he collapsed back in his chair trying to recall the name of this new man of his as it keeps escaping him for some damn reason and King will be damned if he can remember the man's name.

King is having trouble reconciling himself to what the single hero had wrought despite the obstacles put in his way. He feels let down by the forces alleged to be aligned to him for not thwarting this hero earlier mad at the two dirty cops who were proving more inept than dangerous and even Joey Bones, who'd been unable to alter the hero's course.

King had been forced to resort to calling upon the thin man who clearly had not taken care of the hero either as evidenced by his showing up at King's door. King's mad himself for ever trusting the thin man or relying on him and his strange ways. King was still being careful of saying the man's name lest her hear it and come to answer it, hell, most times he didn't want to even think it too loud as who knows how far the man's powers might stretch. King had good cause to be wary of the man showing both good sense and a healthy dose of fear and respect for whatever the thin man's abilities.

King put the thin man out of his mind, he didn't want to know where the man had gotten to or his reasons for letting the hero live. The thin man was too spooky an individual for King to delve too deep or close to any of the reasons the man had for what he did or did not do. King had been well aware during the time of their association how the thin man was working for himself and never King, and working to his own ends with King as his conduit for however long it suited him.

King couldn't focus on his thirst for revenge upon the hero through the pain hazed through whiskey and painkiller.

He'll table it for now as he faces one last unpleasant task before him and one which he has already put off too damned and near unforgivably long, the phone call to Alicia still to be made.

The Last Late Night Call

King last task to complete is weighing on him. He knows he has to make the call regardless hoe he'd really rather not have to. He fully expected the call to be a singularly unpleasant experience as he had to call the deadliest creature he knows, Joey Bones' half-sister Alicia Bonnamo. Her given name then, which had been changed to something else when she'd left all of the wonders of this behind her to travel the world. King's one of only two, pardon one of one now what with the untimely departure of the aforementioned Joey Bones who knows her by this name although he's not certain he still has a right to call her by any name.

He grins slightly as he remembers how particular she was about the way to pronounce her name Alicia. She wanted it enunciated as Ah-lee-cee-ah and was not shy about correcting those who got it wrong and which was not a recommended experience as Alicia was the one with the hot temper in the family. She and Joey Bones were only a little more than a year apart in age, same mother different fathers neither one in sight as they grew up together. Because their circumstances were hard the two had become very close growing up, like creepy close. Joey Bones had turned his talents in a career field where he could support Alicia so she could go to school and eventually get out of the Crescent.

King's trying to remember what her New York City name is, as he knows she changed it as she began her scent to rich and famous. Her photo in those magazines clogging the racks at the local store and seemingly all over the internet too along with information no one should ever have of a woman who is a stranger to them. King wonders what Alicia makes of all the attention and snorts back laugh remembering something she used to say when she was younger wondering if it still held. He imagines so, one doesn't have a motto like she did of 'as long as they're paying' and find cause to alter it.

Thinking of this reminds King that her new professional New York City name is Lisha Danner King recalls it had been a conscious choice on her part to choose this name. It's also a reminder of how she's a long way from this place now, farther away in more than just miles and years measured too.

He checks his watch to see what time it is and sees it's already way past late and still he knows he has to make the phone call to her. She'd never forgive him otherwise and hell, she still might for the delay between the time of death and the call made. An unforgivable interval no matter his fairly legitimate excuse of shot himself, he knows it is still without forgiveness in the mind of one Alicia Bonnamo no matter what she calls herself now.

King hates to be making the call no matter the hour but also knows he has little choice in the matter though so, the time be damned he makes the required phone call. Somewhere in a chic part of New York City a phone rings in a large empty loft with great views. The phone rings a very long time with no sign of being picked up by her or a machine and he's about to give up when it's picked up and he hears a voice he long ago new but now sounds slightly harsh, hoarse.

"Joey's gone right?" Her husky, raspy says into his ear by way of a greeting when she picks up the phone giving King a pause as he wonders how she could know it was him with this news on the line past the 504 on the caller ID. It's an unsatisfactory answer but will have to do King decides still paused unaccustomed to her directness. Typically an answer would have been provided already, a confirmation one way or the other but he finds himself still stuck in the rut of the now uncomfortable silence.

"Lucien," she says using the name she'd known him under way back when and long before he'd chosen King as his moniker. "Tell me what's happened to my Joey Lucien."

Her voice is smooth if agitated and free from the accent he knows she once had but now all but gone King realizes.

"Joey's gone Alicia," King manages to say followed by a long silence from the other end of the line, King wondering if she's gone he cannot see her crying or screaming or any other histrionics on her part. It wouldn't have been the Alicia he remembered anyway and still, he shifts on his feet uncomfortable in the silence.

"Alicia," he questions into the silent space, are you still there, he asks again into the empty space listening for any sign of a response or presence while shifting uncomfortably in it. He has an answer now, knows that using her name was a mistake the minute it passes his lips and one he's sure to pay for it too.

"I'll be down tomorrow Lucien," the voice says followed by a click with King left hanging on the line wondering at what he'd just done.

Jack Kelly

PART II: The Widow's Black

Hell hath no fury like a woman scorned

William Congreve - 1697

Burying Bones

King's standing at the service with his arm up in a sling and his shoulder still aching in a fulfillment of the promise the doc had warned him about. Throbbing like it doesn't have forever to wait to remind him of the pain promised to him from the permanent wound. Not enough pain though to keep his mind from wondering where Alicia is as he hasn't seen her yet and the service is almost over.

Alicia is there the next day as she'd told King she would be, she felt no need to see King first and was in no hurry for the funeral either. She arrives late to it because she didn't want to see Joey like that. It was not how she preferred to remember him all up in a box. She knows it's a selfish thing just like she knows it isn't Joey there in the box either, not her Joey at any rate, so she considers it a fair trade made.

She hides her anger well down deep in her psyche over the selection of service. She doesn't know if its' some residual Irish Catholicism catching up to Joey or if it was King's decision. She decides it doesn't matter as she's still displeased with King for the church service. She doesn't mind the second line to follow though, this is New Orleans after all and it simply wouldn't do to have gone without it, she smiles knowing how her Joey would have insisted on it given a choice. He's always had an appreciation for those kinds of traditions unique to their homeland of the city called New Orleans.

The second line is forming up when she arrives fashionably late, a custom and habit ingrained from all of her years in New York and a carryover from her youth spent here in the Crescent City where nothing starts on time. King is worrying over where she is at, certain she will be here, curious why she hasn't shown herself already and pay her respects if nothing else. The girl he used to know way back when wouldn't behave like this, but then King remembers Alicia

Bonnamo is no longer the girl he remembers but a woman he doesn't know at all.

King has been keeping an eye out for her nervous at her expected arrival without necessarily understanding why at first til he realizes he is bracing for whatever she brings. He expects anger from her, spite too and however these things are multiplied when grief over the sudden death of a loved one with King ignoring the rumors which would make the previous statement have two meanings. King would not give the rumors credence, a form of willful blindness or the knowledge hoe some things are best not known, another lesson from his days as a street soldier.

Alicia appears suddenly at King's shoulder where he can just make her out of the corner of her eye. She stands tall dressed in a widow's black dress complete with a veil to cover her face as well as a black lace parasol over her shoulder. Even her hands are in black lace gloves. King dares to glance at her to get a better look at her and notices she's in black from head to foot including killer heels and hose on her feet and legs. King's thinking about his earlier assessment of her being very far from this place is confirmed by her choice of clothing here.

Alicia's choice of the widow's black is an odd choice and lends credence to the rumors unseemly and dark, gives substantiation to the rumors circulating about how Alicia and Joey Bonnamo had been a little closer than perhaps called for as half siblings no matter their upbringing. King wonders if Alicia cares what her wearing of the widow's black might be interpreted as and then engages in some counter-intuitive thinking and deciding she knew and had done it as a deliberate provocation.

Joey Bones, for his part, had only rarely talked about Alicia Bonnamo. It was a subject which was not to be broached with him and others were well advised to not ask him about or pry too closely about it, and should a deterrent be needed away from this course of conversation it was best to recall how his nickname *was* Bones after all, and his fearsome reputation had been well earned over the years.

Her black hair is long and straight underneath the pinned on veil leaving King wondering if Alicia's still has the faint smattering of freckles across the bridge of her nose and her high cheek bones as a notice of her Irish heritage though he cannot tell past the veil and the powder she most certainly wears. King had forgotten how tall Alicia was especially in heels, near as tall as he was feeling self-conscious now as she turns and is looking him in his eyes.

"Lucien," she says in a low voice as the proceedings demanded without turning to look at him, "tell me about this hero of yours who killed my Joe."

King says nothing for the moment as they continue on following the second line behind the casket. She's looking straight ahead and twirling her parasol lazily with an easy turn of her hands at her shoulder. King's taking a closer look at Alicia Bonnamo, as close as he dares if obliquely. She sounds differently in person, the changes in here more evident now, the distance in years and miles show in the way she walks and how her accent is all but gone replaced with a New York cadence now King notes.

King had suspected she would want vengeance for the loss of Joey Bones though no more than King himself he'd presumed. An incorrect presumption as it turns out with Alicia getting right to business asking about the hero and soon to make it clear she has no interest in being dissuaded from seeking it herself.

King doesn't have to be told this as he could read the seriousness in her eyes. He'd had no intention of even making the attempt to talk her out of it anyway as he begins to tell Alicia what he knows about the hero. Critically he mentions the hero's weakness for blondes as evidenced by the stripper who'd been the catalyst however inadvertent or unknowing behind the hero's actions. King leaves out most of the details of his own involvement even glosses over Joey Bones' suggestion in a sideways fashion for using the girl to get to the hero.

King almost feels for the poor dumb bastard who is now solidly lined up in Alicia Bonnamo's sights. He wasn't certain exactly how she was going to go about it, thinking perhaps she knew herself what her intentions were but he'd be wrong there. He might even be surprised to know how he himself had provided Alicia with what she felt was the key to the hero's destruction.

Alicia envisions herself as one of The Furies, a classic goddess of vengeance in the Greek traditions. Sees herself as Tisiphone the punisher, the avenger of murders and she had her sights solidly set on the hero. The slow destruction as she has no plans to kill the hero quickly or soonest, she wants to punish him first, steal his heart and leave him bereft as only the false love of a woman could accomplish.

Alicia has no intent on sharing her plans with King either, as far as she's concerned, he's already had his chance and blew it. Hell she half thinks he's at fault for her Joey's fate and considers this into her calculations as well and they do not include using or working with King at all. He'd already failed once as she's already observed and it had cost Joey his life. It was the wrong man dead Alicia felt and barely contained the thought every time she talked to or looked at King as she tried hard to tamp down her resentment for.

Alicia Bonnamo will soon prove all too vividly to King and the hero too just how dangerous a creature she really was with repercussions ringing out far and wide in a twist of how these things are usually played out. She smiles as she well knows King and the other peripheral characters involved had no idea coming. First things first she well knew and was focused in on, deal with the hero and everything else after.

Blondeness

Jackie leaves Sissy's place on Burgundy and heads down to the Café Du Monde for some coffee and beignets while he gets his bearings trying to decide where to start in his efforts to find the man called King. Jackie Boy's hoping the combination of the strong coffee and sweets will help to wash away the lingering effects of Sissy's coming to stay the night.

Jackie Boy's contemplating his options for finding the man called King and realizing he had precious few which can be acted upon. He's leaning towards going to the strip club, pardon, *gentlemen's* club and look up Terry as a possible quickest, shortest route way to learn the man called King's whereabouts. Jackie doesn't presume the man is in a hospital or back in his lair where Jackie had forced the shoot out so where to begin otherwise the question He considered it his best possibility as he cannot think of any other options off the top of his head except for the Tweedles, and he'd rather not encounter them for all kinds of reasons which leaves Terry at the strip club pardon *gentlemen's* club as a good place to start.

He gets up and begins to head towards Canal to where the club is located to rout Ol' Terry. Jackie Boy's not worried about the early hour of the day, early by strip club standards, pardon, *gentlemen's* club standards. He figures worst case scenario word will get back to the man called King about his visit and bring King to him or his minions loosed to fetch Jackie Boy to the King. Either way worked out for what Jackie Boy had in mind.

He's moving down Decatur Street when he catches sight of a familiar looking blonde flashing through the crowd on the sidewalks and ahead of him

She has long blonde hair with either a tired out or possibly bad dye job or an old one as you can see the dark roots aligned along the top of her head, the hair is long enough length for hand tossed to fit though it is worn in a style which Sissy never wore. A look which spoke of professional high end care which Sissy hadn't bothered with. Still, there are enough similarities there to produce an uncanny difference which is both a simple enough of and not of a difference to confuse which of course is possibly the entire point of the exercise should he feel like heeding any warning signs.

Jackie has a song stuck in his head at the moment, a song playing like a warning starting from its title on through the lyrics. Curious as to why it should play now, a song playing through his head like some form of warning about the danger prevalent in walking blonde cyphers. The hazards of pursuing blondes with vestiges of coldness about their persona even at this distance, hearts of stone as the damned song in his head, what the hell song is it? He cannot recall until he catches another glimpse of her, Willie DeVille the singer singing of the dangers of any woman who owns a heart of stone. A theory as yet unproven as Jackie cannot get close enough to her to get an accurate reading of her and can only watch as she continues to walk away from him juts out of reach.

Her build is about right if on a taller frame but her gait is all wrong. She walks by placing one foot in front of the other like a dancer he imagines but with the purpose and pace of a New York City woman who means business in her black dress and black heels on black stocking clad legs the kind with the line down the back which used to speak to their authenticity but he doesn't know if it holds any longer either.

Everything about her seems modern and yet also pulled from different parts of the past like her haircut and the stockings she wears. Her dress and the string of pearls about her neck and probably the heels are definitely this century or at least as far as Jackie Boy can identify correctly these kinds of things.

He continues to follow her to get a better look at her, trying to memorize everything about her so he can catalog it for later comparison or contrasting with his memory befogged and clouded still with the remnants of Sissy's last night visit. This blonde is wearing big sunglasses which hide most of her face. She carries a too small purse for usefulness, like the type used for a society party though this is the wrong hour of the day for it. Her right wrist is encircled by a string of white pearls to match the necklace which bounces off of the front of her tight black dress.

Jackie watches her as she makes her way through the crowded street easily as people move out from in front of her so as to give her clean passage, as if it would be anything other than foolish to cross paths with this creature or to impede her in any way shape fashion or form despite the absence of any obvious reason for this. She walks with purpose, a strict means business manner of walking which feels unusual as compared to the native New Orleans unhurried stroll. She walks with a serious comportment, a military like stalk in her carriage as she slices through the world like a stiletto or the fabled cut of a katana.

It's effective too as the world parts to allow her to move through untouched and without delay. There's recognition there, however subconscious, of the situation, a form of respect reserved for a predator or other similarly dangerous things moving about the world and allowing them to get where they want to be and doing one's damndest to not attract their attention.

Jackie finds he's mostly mesmerized by her, by her walk even as he's wondering what such an exotic creature as she clearly is, is doing here in the banana republic of New Orleans. Jackie doesn't know why but he feels she's a New York City kind of a gal, it's the vibe he gets off of her, her cool sophistication walking about all in black under the bright hot summer sun of a New Orleans August and unperturbed by it or unwilling to show it.

He's intrigued to the point of distraction by her, something about her which keeps Jackie after her if at a cautionary distance as he suspects she's a lead astray. She's already succeeded in pulling Jackie Boy off his intended course of action Terry and the *gentlemen's* club as he satisfies his need to continue to follow her through the streets of the Quarter on what is feeling more and more like the equivalent of a snipe hunt as he is unable to close the distance with her.

If Jackie had listened more closely he would have heard Sissy imploring him as she had so often to cease what he was doing and come home. Sissy still a faint echo in his head lingering like the damned Willie DeVille song now stuck in his head. Jackie continues to follow this blonde here. She's just similar enough to his lost girl for him to get lost in the pursuit of her, of attempting to separate out the two more clearly in his own mind, if he's able.

He has succumbed to his impulsive obsessiveness despite the warnings clinging to him and his continued inability to presently catch up to her here just yet. He cannot see the secret smile upon Alicia's face at the success already achieved with her first brush at the hero. She's pleased how relatively easy it had been to find him and then to lead him about by using the hero's predilection for blondes against him.

Alicia had been enjoying the prolonged teasing of the hero, of the proof given of his blondeness. Her smile stays as she recalls an ever so important lesson learned from where she cannot recall unless it was simply inherent to her gender. Always leave them wanting more, an important element of the tease as she decides it's time for her to quit the hero and leave him hanging, presumably wanting more and unable to get her out of his mind.

Alicia allows the crowds on the street to close around her and aid in her disappearing act. She abandons the hero there with just the taste the hint of her with the hero well satisfied with herself for the first day's work done. Alicia is pleased with this test of her ability to exploit the hero's weakness. She'll give it a day or two and then she'll move to the second step in her plan of personal peril for the hero. She's already envisioning the next encounter with the hero where she'll seduce the hero further into her web.

Jackie Boy doesn't know how, but he has lost the blonde to the crowds. One minute she'd been there, the next she had not like she'd willed it to happen. Jackie almost feels like she's plotted out the whole thing to ensnare Jackie, another alarm going off from a more rational section of Jackie's brain, unfortunately ringing muted and mostly unheard.

Jackie decides to try to put this blonde out of his mind, to try and to shake her and the lingering image of her walk and the way she carried herself. An image and a memory too impressed to be rapidly dimmed and this effort mostly ineffective and threatening to linger.

Lucien and Lisha

Alicia returns from her jaunt with the hero satisfies with her test of what King had told her the man's weakness were. She hadn't far to travel from the Quarter back to where she had taken up residence in Joey's place. It was her inheritance now however sorrowful the thought might be and she'd always had a key to it after all even if she hadn't been to it in years.

Thankfully though this is not the old homestead back in the channel, there are too many old memoires there and most of those unpleasant too. Alicia was glad he'd moved out of it, left it behind for this nice clean condo in the CBD which looks out over Julia Street. It's a quiet part of the city here and she has left the place mostly untouched though not out of any morbidity or thoughts of preserving it like as shrine or some such, so much as she'd been too busy attending to the hero and her plot against him to bother with any rearranging of the place. She's worry about it if she decided to stay a decision as yet still unmade and too far in the future to worry about presently.

Alicia hadn't moved in to Joey Bone's place because of any touch of sentimentality on her part as it wasn't an attribute of hers other than for her need for a place of privacy where she could mourn her loss. She'd moved in because it was hers by right now and because she needed a place to stay while she executed her plans against the hero.

Alicia would cry later though when she was well enough alone and her task completed. Right now she was focused in on her revenge against those who had wronged her. This included the plans she had for King as well. She blamed him just as much if not more for the loss of her Joey and had thoughts of steering the hero back at King in a delicious form of irony or perhaps dèjà vu. Ultimately though she'd decided she much rather preferred the satisfaction of vengeance by her own hand, a desire to see the look in each man's eye when they realized what she'd wrought. The fulfilling of the role she had in mind for herself as a Furies, as Tisiphone the avenger as she sought redress for the loss of her love Joey Bonnamo because somebody had to pay for the crime of her beloved of her beloved's death and she had two men in mind.

Alicia soaks in the tub indulging in this moment as she internally steels herself for her next move. Tomorrow she'll visit King for a twofold purpose, the first to reveal her new look, to reintroduce herself as Lisha Danner and to set some things straight with him as her secondary purpose, to explain to the man how she wasn't going to wait on him to solve the hero and to leave it to her.

She also intends to poke the bear, as it were, to see what and how King will react to her assertiveness in the matter of the hero. Alicia wants to goad King into overplaying his hand while revealing some of the inner workings and assets of his organization or what's left of it so she might slip in behind him with his attention focused elsewhere until too late he realizes she has taken everything from him. She sees it as a furtherance of her role as the punisher and avenger of the murdered, a payback for those who have caused the death of her Joey.

She arrives unannounced at King's offices the next day, walking in like she owned the place. His office is still in a state of recovered shambles. The room is still pock marked in its desk and walls with the bullet holes from the gun battle and a barely covered stink of cordite and blood stale still permeating the office. Alicia manages to take in everything around her with a practiced look of boredom on her face honed to sharp perfection on the runways and photoshoots of her New York life and career.

She can feel King watching her as she examines the room finding it and its owner wanting in an assessment already predetermined. She's simply seeking confirmation now of the kind of man Lucien is now, wanting to see how far he too had come, how far removed like she herself was from the days when he'd not pretended to a name like King.

"Alicia," King says to her back causing her to turn and stare the coldest hardest stare he's ever personally seen let alone received at him. Her attitude is practiced casual but there's a real tension there in the way she walks which combines with the stare to give King pause as a sharp chill dances up his spine.

"Call me Lisha, Lucien," she says to him her eyes still looking right at him, pardon through him and he can almost feel her judgment of finding him wanting. It is not a comfortable place for him to be. She has purposefully called him Lucien he thinks, a reminder from her of how he too used to be somebody else and never mind the ironic quality when she insists on using her new name while denying him the use of his. It's an unpleasant reminder he thinks, a little jab from her about pretexts and of pretending at aspirations unsecured.

She tells him he is to never use the name Alicia with her anymore without further explanation though it's fairly clear he has either lost or had the privilege of pretending he knew her when revoked. He understands it really as it isn't who she is anymore, and hasn't been in a very long time. She *is* Lisha Danner from her clothes to her hair to her walk and attitude so it was best he get used to the idea and probably soonest.

She most certainly wasn't Alicia any longer, so Lisha Danner would do King thought. He took an extra minute now to watch her stalk about his office for a stalk is what it most certainly was and he realized with a twinge he was clearly amongst her intended prey. This was a new threat King thought, clearly reading the warning signs from the predator in his presences knowing it recognizing it for the toying it was making King's earlier assertation of her as the most dangerous creature prescient.

This woman before him in his office now is a woman whom King has never seen the like of before. King's stunned and rightly worried by the power he can feel radiating outward from her, whether from anger or something else he cannot tell but it is exuded in both her new look and her attitude.

King's well aware of having told Alicia, pardon Lisha, about the hero and blondes but he certainly hadn't expected this from her, could not have been prepared for her having dyed her hair blonde, for having taken what he'd told her as the hero's weakness so seriously as to have committed to this dye job clearly prepared to stake herself out as the bait in the trap set for the hero. King's surprised at her dedication to the task at hand, if uncertain what to make of it exactly except as a quick reminder to King of the tinge of predator and prey he'd felt only a moment before.

King watches her a little longer as she stands in his office before his desk. King is thinking how the dying of her hair, the emphasized insistence on being called Lisha, her New York name, even her standing her were all measures of a thing being purposefully done and done for reasons other than the downfall of the hero. He feels himself squarely in her sights, as it were. The question hinting around wanting to be asked of her is how far past the hero is she aiming for.

King's feeling nervous and unsure under her gaze even when it does not fall directly upon him. He's waiting for her to speak he realizes, to say something of the reason why she had come to pay him a visit. Unless her statement has already been made in her blonde hair, her widow's black, and her silence which still seems to hold contempt within it for the men she blames for the loss of her Joey. King can feel her silently accusing him of not being capable prior or going forward of dealing with the hero as he shifts in his chair suddenly very aware of the pills and the glass of whiskey in front of him and a need to break the silence between the two of them.

"Alicia," King begins before catching himself, "Lisha." he asks in a testing the air type query, not certain what he wants to ask her other than why she's here in his office. She looks up and over to him and he's almost sorry now to have drawn her attention.

"Lisha," he begins again and feels an ease however slight cross her body as she stands across the room from him.

"For the hero," he asks her raising his one good hand to the side of his head in a gesture to mean her hair's new color, the blonde is for the hero?

She only smiles a crooked smile being enigmatic as she moves about King's barely put back together office. King swears he can almost hear her tsk-tsking in disapproval as she moves in a panther like grace on her high heels. She steps to his desk and lifts his glass of whiskey in her hands and to her lips before pausing there.

"No need for you to worry about it anymore Lucien." is her reply as she pours down the drink and wipes the corner of her mouth with the back of her hand her smile grown out a little haughtier.

"It's already in the works Lucien," she says turning to look at him across her shoulder as she stands sideways to him with the cryptic smile still on her face as she looks at Lucien. She flat refuses to use his adopted moniker of King as she felt it was a pretentious use by him especially in light if his failures with the hero as evidenced by the state of his office and of himself as well, an injured arm pinned to his chest in a sling all pointing to weakness and vulnerability.

King feels suddenly self-conscious of his wounded and mostly useless arm raiding his other hand to it to absently rub an ache from it which according to the docs would never go completely away pain killers or not. The docs had told King the arm never would again be one hundred percent and had not listed an optimistic percentage of usability for King either.

King doesn't think to offer it as an excuse to her though, he senses it would not be well received in the present state of mind she appeared to be in and he reminded himself how he did not know this person despite her proximity in appearance to a person he once had. A person long gone now and a stranger before him and he best tread carefully in this new territory.

King thinks to protest her decision or to implore her to leave the hero to him. Some explanation of how it was his responsibility as the King of the city, as Joey Bones' boss and friend and as a man to see to the hero. He thinks to tell her to trust him in this endeavor but decides not to say any of it to her figuring it all as a waste of time.

"Thanks for the drink," Lisha says to him as she sets the glass down on his desk her hand on top of it and seemingly screwing it down tighter into the desk top. She seems to be looking right through him and deciding something about him. She rises to her full height on her killer heels and barks out a scoff, turning in her widow's black dress and walking out of his office and releasing the pressure her presence had filled the room with.

King's relieved with her exit and the built up tension he'd felt in Lisha Danner's presence. Like she'd sucked up all of the oxygen in the room and had left precious little left over for King to breath. He feels like a weight has been removed from his chest as he reaches for the glass she'd used and picks it up to see her lipstick smudge on its room and he throws it across the room to smash against the far fall.

He's angry with himself for his inability to confront her over her choices being made and of her behavior in his office. He'd let the fear of near death take hold of him and had allowed her to dominate the center of his empire. She must have sensed his fear somehow, detected in her predatory state which would explain her scoffing at him and of shutting him out of whatever she had planned for the hero.

Through his anger, King puts the fear aside and begins to rally himself to action feeling a pressing need to get out ahead of Lisha Danner before it all came back on him somehow. He closes the cap on the pills and the whiskey knowing he's going to need to stay sharp if he's going to beat her as they were to be adversaries now, kill or be killed the message she'd sent as she'd paced his office and the only warning she was going to give him.

King would end the hero and reclaim his place as the rightful and only King of the city and not even Alicia Lisha or whatever the fuck she chooses to call herself was going to take what he'd built and like the hero almost had. He

King has only a brief precautionary and fleeting thought as to what consequences he might face if he should deny her the vengeance she sought. He decides he couldn't and wouldn't worry about it he felt a small matter of his own survival at this point in time, deciding in the same moment considering Lisha's issued warning that if she should get in the way he wouldn't hesitate to kill her too.

Döppelblonder

This time Jackie doesn't have to stumble upon the blonde or try to follow her through a crowd. This time the blonde comes right up to Jackie as he sits just inside the door of one of his favorite drinking spots down low in the Quarter. A pint of amber in his hands only just started upon as he mulls his unsuccessful bid so far to track down the man called King to exact his revenge.

The blonde walking with her purposeful walk dressed in black seemingly oblivious to the heat large sunglasses on her face like the actress use to famously wear circa the late 1960's or so. Her lips are red and a string of white pearls sit tight at her throat as she walks up to him her moves unwavering and unhesitant with a surety to herself expressed through her body and the way she moves and holds herself of a fashion of complete control.

She stops when she sees our hero and pauses to purse her lips as she raises a black gloved hand to her sunglasses and carefully casually practiced pulls them down a bit to reveal her eyebrow, eyelid and the top portion of her eye as she looks over the rim of the glasses at him. Jackie is frozen for the moment caught in her stare and feeling like prey must when confronted with its natural predator.

She sits down without invitation on the next bar stool over signaling the bartender to order herself a drink. She waits for it to be delivered and takes a sip before she turns and boldly faces our hero. The blonde of her hair is like a faint reminder of the lost girl to Jackie, like a haunt though this woman is feeling more a Döppelblonder to him than anything more substantially real as odd a feeling as this statement feels in his brain.

"Hello stranger," the blonde woman says to him and her resemblance to the lost girl is lost the minute she does so giving Jackie Boy the time to pause and take all of her in. This woman before him other than being blonde is not at all like the lost girl, any likeness coming from a confusion created by his brain still smudged with a tinge of the effects of the late night dream which had caused him to do so. The wishful similarity straight pulled from the files of wishful thinking, purposeful misleading to confuse this blonde for the lost girl when he should well know it is so much impossibility.

Jackie's a little surprised to find her sitting here across from him, hadn't expected her to walk his way again thinking it so much coincidence to have another blonde cross his path, especially so soon after the girl lost. She tells him it's lucky they've meet like this. It's said with a sly smile as she turns her attention away from him, pretending too hard she's not her for him at all and mostly interested in her drink and possibly some passably conversation of a mostly transitory nature if he's able.

She of course knows how luck had nothing to do with her being here with him as she concentrates on her drink. She'd made this chance encounter happen through her own diligence as the next step in her plan against the hero. Jackie Boy hears what she has said though it doesn't register. If he'd had more presence of mind he'd have cringed at this use of the word luck knowing he personally only had the one kind even if it was presently on a serious hot streak.

Jackie's still stuck in his surprise at her presence here next to him let alone her actually speaking to him. He has a strong desire to see more of her eyes still covered and hidden behind her large sunglasses. He's wondering what color her eyes are and what secrets they might tell if he could look into them, the whole windows to the soul theory. The thought makes Jackie turn his eyes away from her to stare into his pint of beer as he tries to read the signs in the clings of foam along the sides of the glass waiting to slide back down in inevitable surrender to gravity to be reclaimed by the beer still there.

Her name is Lisha Danner she tells him, continuing on talking to him like there isn't any awkwardness in the space between them, like they're not strangers after all to one another. Lisha works to draw him out with her carefully calculated statements, an interplay of flirting and tease and open spaces wot allow him to interpret things for himself. She's frankly a little surprised and a little stymied how the hero hasn't risen to the bait of it yet and wonders what she has to do to sweeten the pot a bit more or if she should leave and try another chance encounter a little later on.

She wonders if her directness has put the hero off or if he too was feeling the near impossibility of her sitting here as being an encounter by happenstance. She hates it but she is stumped for a moment as she tries to determine her next move her pride a little hurt at lack of success presently.

Jackie Boy can see the blonde sitting next to him of course, could smell her perfume hell, he could reach out and touch her if he wanted to and he still wasn't quite certain she was real. He still has his mind traveling back to the girl even with this other blonde now before him or the catalyst the faint reminder of what once was and the cause for his mind wandering off course when it never really needed much of a prompt normally anyway.

"So," she declares bringing Jackie's attention squarely back to her and the present, "care to show this stranger around?"

Lisha on a different tact now taking a more direct path at the hero remembering this man's affinity for strippers, pardon *exotic* dancer. He looks over at her and she seals his fate or at least ends his debate about should or shouldn't when she removes her sunglasses holding them by the earpiece in her right gloved hand as she turns to look at him. Jackie Boy gets lost in the deep pools of her eyes, eyes which are a very cool yet still radiant blue and somehow seemed to have the power to both see right through you and yet still tell her every one of your little secrets to her.

Somehow Jackie Boy understands this is a gift of sorts though potentially one of a dubious nature like a Greek horse as well as a rarity seldom offered up by her. He doesn't know it yet and he won't for a time longer as she's seldom without her sunglasses or he mostly sees her in the dark which mutes the power of her blue eyes. Though he will never forget the straight ice cold chill her eyes send down to the very base of his spine lending a new definition to the term cold to the bone, the kind of cold which once felt you don't ever forget and this from only the initial glacial stare of hers unmatched by her sly grin and body language with promises of sin writ large and in a common language.

He doesn't hear himself say yes or agree to go with her, a mostly moot point to dwell on as he's standing next to her as they move on down the street paying no attention to their surroundings, eyes only for each other as they feel the crackle of the electricity between them. Jackie's feeling ensorcelled by her though unable to alter the present trajectory, lost in the moment, in a blur of blonde.

He tells himself he's moving though not entirely of his own will to do so. He tells himself he's still befuddled by the dreams of the lost girl and this blonde while a faint reminder of her and different from Sissy in all kinds of ways is still close enough if he can have her just one last time. He's caught somewhere in this in-between space of close enough and not caring either. All lies, he wants this wants to be here and has no interest in altering any trajectory for whatever reason despite reservations and clear klaxon like warnings from multiple sources. A desire for destruction as the Mistress had pointed out, as the girl herself had and many others as well, and Jackie Boy once again paying none if it any mind in a live for today moment generously accredited to his thinking here.

He doesn't recall the trip to wherever they end up at all as the next moments pass in a blur, a whirlwind spin through steps and streets taken to a destination at once familiar and foreign. As they walk they pause to succumb to the crackle of heat and electricity they feel between them, they tug at each other's clothes and bodies interrupted by bursts of remembrance of being in public and really wanting, desiring, needing privacy for what they're about to do with and to each other. They reach an unmarked doorway and crash through to the interior of a darkened house.

"Don't you want me," she asks coy all of a sudden, a smile from over her shoulder as she stands and moves away from him for a moment, standing in front of him but stepping away and increasing the distance between them in this strange surrealistic dream. A place where you know time is passing but you don't know how much or how quickly. Near completely unaware of the ticking unable to feel the earth moving on its axis beneath you and hoping, only hoping mind you that she's somehow experiencing it too.

"You have to say you want me Jackie," she says to him still moving away from him with her movements deliberately slow, sinuous and sexy.

Jackie moves towards her and embraces her in the doorway pressing her against the door. She shuffles them into the room and they fall into bed together tangled in delight like it's a natural conclusion, like something which had already been decided upon and the two of them had been simply going through the motions of a construct which called for an appropriate waiting period before committing to the action desired all along.

They move together in perfect practiced synchronicity, and move in conjoined tandem as if they've done it for ages silently towards the same goal, the same idea and destination. No words are spoken no directions necessary, simply an effortless lock step type of an operation as she moves before him reaching back with her hand to take his and lead him as he willingly follows not daring to think or wonder at what happens next. He's simply hoping and open to any idea which presents itself figuring he would be pleased with whatever it might be.

They reach the bedroom dark except for the light from the street streaked through the shutters and uneven where they finally break their hand hold and allow for a small separation to form between them to form a pause and the last chance to alter any possible procedures. She moves before him and unbuckles the belt of his jeans letting them fall to the ground standing still a moment before reaching beneath her short hairdo to do her magical bra removal thing without taking off her dress which all girls learn to do. She pulls her bra out from under her dress before taking a hesitant step or two to kiss him lightly on the lips before she descends to lie in the bed with enough space cleared for one more. He steps out of his jeans and kicks them to the side as he lifts his shirt up and off before kneeling on the edge of the bed to lean in and kiss her.

Her arms reach up to engulf and draw him in to her warmth as he crawls in to the space next to her to intertwine in her long, long legs and arms. She's still wearing her string of white pearls tight at her throat and nothing else except the bedsheets which is somehow even sexier. He feels the warmth of her body losing himself there despite all the warnings against it, her kiss persuading him otherwise as they slip into the embrace of the night and of course just absolutely incredible sex.

The hero and the blonde lay next to each other as the sweat from their combined efforts settles and cools on their bodies tangled in the sheets. Both parties are keeping their thoughts to themselves for the moment as they recover their senses from the initial session. The hero sits up and sweeps his feet over the edge of the bed sitting there for a moment as Lisha looks over at him and sees the airborne tattoo on his right shoulder and she smiles a secret smile at this second truth found beyond his weakness for blondes as she bites into his shoulder eliciting an ow from the hero much to her private pleasure.

Just playing she says out loud inside secretly enjoying the first strike against the hero though it does give Jackie Boy pause as he looks Lisha Danner over once more trying to see the real her and unable to do so. Her arms wrapped around his shoulders her lips planting small kisses on his shoulder and whispers in his ear to come back to bed with her and he lets her weight carry them both back down to the waiting sheets.

Jackie Boy later reluctantly rises from the tangle of sweat soaked sheets hazed and unsure but lying next to her had felt like contentment for a moment until he'd made the mistake of taking a closer look at the blonde in hand and realized it was not his lost blonde, not his girl at all. He wonders if this counts as betrayal, if this is him breaking a promise made or not as he doesn't quite know if the dead can still hold a person to a promise made or not, or if these are the singular promises which a person should ever be expected to be held to or obligated to when they're the only party left to the agreement.

A lot to think about in the deep night as he rummages through the fridge for a beer and drinks it down trying hard to avoid any thinking at all before returning to the bed and his new blonde now. She's lying on face down and away from him and her hair has fallen in a fashion which allows him to make out a tattoo up high on the back of her neck right beneath the hair line, a tattoo which should not be there and now he knows for certain this is a Döppelblonder and not his at all.

He doesn't let go of her though, he prefers to stay pretending for another moment longer not willing to let the evening go just yet, not ready to surrender her back to anything. He settles in on his back as his hand finds a pleasant purchase on the lovely little cleft and rise of her ass cheek comforting in the dark as she lies on her stomach head turned underneath the pillow with her hair splayed out in odd curls. She dozes lightly a self-satisfied grin on her face for the completion of this part of her plan to undo the hero as well as some really fun sex had.

Jackie's not sleeping tonight, knows it's nothing more than a long promised elusive chase unfinished and all he can do now is wait the night to move on towards its rendezvous with the dawn knowing one of them will be gone before the other wakes and his money is on the blonde.

King's Horses

King was chewing on another pain pill with a whiskey accompanying in an effort of trying to tamp down both his anger and his pain competing against each together and yet seeming to also work together to torment him. King's list of torments range from the death of Joey Bones to the damned tall thin man not killing the sorry sonnaofabitch want to be hero complete with his seeming absence from the scene in his litany of grievances. King didn't know where the tall thin man had gotten to and certainly wasn't about to go looking for the man, especially in his weakened state as he somehow instinctively knew that the tall thin man would feast on his present weakened state and he already had his hands full with one Alicia Bonnamo.

King didn't like the feeling of being sidelined in his own city, didn't like Alicia striking out on her own to deal with the problem of the hero complete with her turn to blonde. King thought it an indication of how Alicia was thinking King couldn't handle the problem. This theory was aided by the combination of his being wounded, his office being shot to pieces and Joey Bones' dead as arguments in favor of this working theory.

King felt almost thankful to Alicia or Lisha as she was calling herself presently for the glimpse into her cold and calculating nature. For the display of a most deadly calm which made her most frightful and fearsome for the power it gave her and she was showing nearly natural proclivity for it. Her display had King thinking he'd better watch his ass around her when she's in this frame of mind. King felt it was a proper amount of fear of her as he felt it was just as likely she's going to kill him at the end of all this and it was best to be prepared.

He hated to admit to it because of the hint of weakness it implied, but he was doubly unnerved by Alicia Bonnamo. First by how she had known what he had to say on the phone all the way in New York City and her swift appearance here in the

Crescent City. Alicia's decision to go blonde, after he had told her of the man's seeming weakness for the type had paled the first issue, King's perplexed by Alicia's interpretation of becoming the blonde woman needed to destroy the man whose dedication towards hero shit had resulted in Joey Bones death and her presence here in the Crescent City of her birth.

He's struggling too with her insistence on being called by her New York name of Lisha Danner when he still sees her as Alicia Bonnamo, Joey Bones little sister from when they were all still young. It's a thought and a memory he has to be careful of lest he get sentimental or forgetful and then doesn't put her down if she should get in the way of his goal of reclaiming his city and his position near its top as King just like Walken had in the movie which he so admired.

King was feeling a pressing needed to get out in front of this one, put his anger at being shot up to the side. He needed to forget how close he felt he'd come with the next life and to quit chewing on the details of the events and focus in on the business at hand. King needed to put his personal stake, his need for revenge aside as he could not afford or allow himself to be turned into a cliché. Return it to being business and kill the hero the first chance he got. Then he could secure his kingdom and move on.

There was no need for anything fancy or cute, he'd leave fancy and cute to Alicia and her now blonde hair, leave Lisha alone to play whatever games she had in mind with the hero. King would take care of business and leave it at that and be done with it as he felt it was critically important how he do it himself or at least be the cause of it, recalling the resistance to succumbing to cliché. He doesn't dare leave it to Lisha not if he ever wants to face her again or reclaim his empire.

He doesn't know why he thinks his luck with this damnded hero would be any different this time as compared to their first encounter but he felt he had to try. His reputation and position as King of the city was at stake and now assailed from two sides, the hero and Lisha and if he let things linger much linger the rest of the members of the local criminal ensemble as well. He remembered how Walken had when necessary taken things into his own hands in the movie King so admired. He was taking these lessons to heart here, if he wanted to be the King, hell at this point if he wanted to retain his position in his own organization he had to do something and soon with precious few options left to him.

He knew all these things fairly clearly and well and was still at a loss about what to do now this pesky hero who refused to die or stop coming after them. King had tried every nasty thing he could think of against the hero including the use of the thin man and all had ended up in disappointment as he racked his brain to come up with a solution to the problem of the hero. He still wanted vengeance for himself and for Joey Bones but mostly he simply wanted to know he was rid if the hero permanently so he could turn his attentions of all of the threats and small fires burning at the edges of his empire including some not near as far away as he'd liked.

No fooling round this time either and just straight shoot the sonnaofabitch and then spit on the grave to make sure you know he's dead. King thinking he might even go to the extreme of a stake through the sonnaofabitch's heart to make sure and then burn the body to ensure there was no chance of any return by the hero ever again. King knew these were primitive actions long ago taken against the dead and he hated he had to turn to them, but such was his frame of mind presently he felt he had cause and need to turn to these to ensure the hero's destruction.

King's still angry over the hero's insistence and persistence. His inability to have left things alone how there'd never have been any reason for the two of them to have had any relation to one another at all. And never mind the troubling thought of how this could have worked in reveres as well, how King himself or his minions could themselves have left well enough alone. If either party had spent or spared two seconds of thought none of this would have had to have been and all parties could've gone on their merry courses all for the want of leaving well enough alone.

He liked the thought of seeing the hero destroyed as he poured himself another glassful of whiskey from the near empty fifth sitting on his desk next to the dwindling pile of pain pills. King remembering he had sworn himself to a closer form of sober than he was presently achieving. His pistol and spare bullets sit nearby in a jarring contradiction against his once beautiful but now bullet riddled cherry wood desk, which had at one time set him back a near small fortune.

He liked the idea of revenge, but how to do it was the question beating round his brain, the tormenting conflict demanding a plan for its resolution. King figured Alicia as the blonde Lisha Danner wouldn't have any trouble flushing the hero out from wherever he was and then King thought, then he could have his troops in play to grab up the hero and deliver him to King so King could finish the poor dumb bastard off once and for all. The more he tossed the idea about the more he liked it especially using Alicia as the bait she apparently wished to be.

King despised weaknesses, and knew Alicia did as well. He knew how his weakened state had already been noticed by those about him and like all predators with an eye to these things they would circle and pounce given the chance for their chance at prey with the keys to the kingdom a secondary thought amongst many of them. It was a thing to be sorted out later though perhaps not for all of them King thought especially of Alicia here.

Alicia whether as herself or in her present guise of Lisha Danner is still the most dangerous person he knew and potentially more so now with the emphasis on her alter ego of Lisha. The use of the name Lisha like a one step aside from her regular persona, or as King thought of it at any rate, which he feared gave her enough distance to do some potentially very nasty things and something to be very, very worried about it. King thought it best to resolve the situation and diffuse Alicia slash Lisha with the demise of the hero and return her to a more benign setting and preferably back to her New York City life and well enough away from him and the city. Each person back to their natural habitat as it were, and at the quickest if possible.

King likes the loose idea he has formed and laughs out loud at the simplicity of it reviving the pain to be washed down by another hit from the fifth. He reaches for the phone with his right hand for the land line phone, knocking the receiver off the hook and then punching in a series of numbers by heart listening for the first ring before picking up the phone and putting it up to his ear.

It's time now for King to rally his troops and martial his resources and all those pseudo military clichés used interchangeably between business and war. He smiles a little at the thought as this situation at any rate was certainly both and always was or had been and something he understood fairly well as a former street level soldier. His smile only widens as he waits for the call he's put out to his pair of dirty cops, the Tweedles in Jackie Boy's parlance and waits to see what his stir causes.

Tweedles

King's pair of dirty cops are a little surprised to have received a call from a man whom according to all last reports had been shot damn near straight to hell or as close to it as a person could get and not stay. It's a short conversation a reiteration of a conversation had only a short amount of days ago. It seems despite all efforts the hero was not only not dead but also still on the loose and still coming for King, feeling like the narration in a movie promo somehow.

King explains in short order what he wants the pair to do giving them the briefest description and explanation of Lisha Danner and her role in the play unfolding. He doesn't ask if they can or are able to do this task, it is simply assumed they can and will as per their previous arrangement and price point. King's hoping the pair will be able enough to tangle with Alicia, pardon Lisha, King still getting used to her conversion to blonde as he ends the call and turns back to his whiskey and pills with nothing now to do but the waiting.

The two cops, the Tweedles as Jackie Boy has always referred to the pair having never bothered to learn their names are detectives Isaac 'Ike' Thompson and Clay Richards. Just how this pair had managed to escape all the purges and investigations of NOPD over the years spoke to some ability of theirs but none were ever sure exactly which as the pair where not held in regard of any kind anywhere in the department.

Still, they were twelve year NOPD veterans and had probably been on the take in one form or another for the entirety of their tenure. It wasn't a moral issue or even a law and order issue, it was simply how things were done and had been done to the point of being nearly expected in NOPD probably since its inception especially in vice where they worked now and never mind the side of the street.

Jackie Boy has just stepped into the Quarter walking back along Decatur near the river from his evening spent with the other blonde. His mind still occupied by the two blondes blurring together imperfectly but never separating enough to clarify the distinction between the two. He's thinking of heading down and getting some coffee and beignets once more hoping the sugar and caffeine are enough to clear some things up in his brain.

Last night's tryst, and no other word for it really, with the other blonde is weighing on Jackie Boy in a strange sensation which seems to hew closely towards guilt or some equivalency. It's not like Jackie Boy has a reference for this point foreign and strange to him and without previous reference point by which to draw comparison.

The thoughts are preoccupying him as he makes his way deeper into the Quarter when he hears a screech of brakes and shouts to get up against the wall coming from behind him. Jackie turns confused to see who it is shouting at him and realizes it is a plague of Tweedles which descend upon him, the pair getting an early start on their cop clichés today. There's something wrong with the picture though which Jackie Boy cannot quite put his finger on and isn't given enough time to finish the thought when they're on top of him.

"Hey there Jackie Boy," The Tweedles say as they each take a side of him and then jam him up against the wall of a nearby building and rabbit punch him in the kidneys a couple of times for old times' sake or some such sentimental reason.

"Nice to see you again Jackie Boy." is said by one of the Tweedles followed by another punch. There's a small pause as the pair let the pain sink into Jackie Boy who is attempting to squint away the stars in his eyes. He only partially succeeds when he realizes what had been wrong with the picture as he'd thought it only a moment before. Jackie realizes what the error is when they spin him back around to face them. The error was how the Tweedles were dressed in plains clothes.

Jackie's a little surprised he hadn't realized NOPD was in such straights as to promote these two schmucks. They must be damned desperate to have done so and then Jackie Boy says what he's thinking out loud before he can stop himself assuming of course it had ever been a possible alternative. He directs it in general at the pair of them as he can still not tell one from the other and had never really bothered to differentiate before and didn't really see any need to do so here either.

"Fuck me," Jackie says, "but I cannot believe they promoted you two assholes!"

The pair of Tweedles look at each other and then back at him as they silently decide what the punishment will be for his smart ass remark.

"That's rich coming from you funny man," one of the pair replied, "a regular comedian here our Jackie Boy," he continues or the other one chimes in. The pair then silently nod their heads in agreement as they work to reward Jackie Boy for his smart ass comment with their fists as one could have rightly predicted as most likely when you're running your mouth. Jackie Boy was not surprised though, not his first go round with this lot as the saying goes and besides the Tweedles were a notoriously humorless lot.

Their punches turn to kicks as Jackie falls to the ground unceremoniously like a sack of shit. An unflattering if apt description as he rolls on his shoulder to his side to hack up and spit out a gouge of blood onto the pavement wondering at how much blood he's donated to the streets of the city over the years as he fights back the rising pain of a situation which is all too familiar for him.

The Tweedles are still saying something to him but he can't make it out past the ringing in his ears. Jackie Boy rolls on to his back bringing him all kinds of new and delightful bouts of pain and stars to his eyes so now he's blind too in an addition to his current pile of fun. One of the Tweedles leans in and grabs Jackie Boy's jaw in his hands squeezing hard and saying something to him which Jackie Boy can only make out in an every other letter kind of way.

"Damn Jackie Boy why don't you ever learn to mind your own business," Tweedle One says out loud to him, to his partner, to no-one really.

"You don't know it Jackie Boy," says the other Tweedle he thinks hard to make out a clear picture past the stars blinking in and out of his vision. "But you are one lucky sonnaofabitch because someone else wants you or we'd be or the taking Jackie Boy on his last ride to nowhere.'

"Strange I don't feel lucky," Jackie says his mouth racing out before any amount of sense or desire for self-preservation. The Tweedles stiffen up a minute in anger and, Jackie swears he can hear them shaking their collective heads at the wonder of it all

"Fucking comediennes," he hears one of them comment followed by a pause as the pair check to see if they've drawn an audience. It is way too early in the day for anyone to pay them any mind as the streets are mostly empty except for stragglers and cleanup crews prepping the city for another round. The Tweedles unleash a quick flurry of blows to his ribcage then to his back when he doubles over and doesn't stop until he's back on his knees on the ground trying hard to not cough up his spleen with one arm around his waist to hold his ribs and guts in place the other hand on the ground to keep his face from off of it.

"Damn smartass," he hears one of the Tweedles say through the ringing in his head and his ears now unsynchronized with each other and creating quite the racket. The ringing in his hears threatening to line up into a right proper cacophony with the pounding in his head.

"We still gotta deliver him alive," says one receiving a snorted grunt from the other as reply and a grumble from the other before agreement is reached by the pair. One of them tells Jackie Boy to get up which Jackie would take as a joke in his present condition were it not this pair delivering the punch line.

They're presently an impatient pair, already out in the open daylight more than they liked as they reach down to grab hum under his armpits and violently assist him to his feet. They steady him between them for a second as they're about to drag his ass to the car for a quick trip to somewhere vastly unpleasant Jackie Boy is thinking.

They take their first steps as one Tweedle says something to the other across Jackie's back and then laughs out loud at his on joke but their voices are lost to him as nothing more than a buzzing line of indecipherability as his eyes roll in his head though not as a together act. He spits out a glob of blood and probably a tooth, hell maybe even part of rib who knows which to enable himself to breath in better sucking in a large breath and choking down a wallop of immense pain as a chaser for big fun.

His focus is mostly gone but one thing the Tweedles had shared with him was how they were operating under someone else's orders. Jackie Boy has a fairly good idea whose orders too and smiles a strange strangled little smile as he realizes he's back on course and no longer having to worry about blondes or any other troubles. The Tweedles here were about to solve a host of problems for him in one fell swoop when they deliver him, he presumes, to the man called King where Jackie Boy can finally enact the revenge he's sought after for more than a little while now. He smiles because after chasing cross half the city and to death's door and back here he was about to be served up with almost no effort on his part.

Another stretch of your famous bad luck streaks there, eh Jackie, one or the other of the Tweedles says as he reaches for the car door when they're interrupted by an authoritative shout which catches the Tweedles attention. This same voice follows up with more, but Jackie Boy cannot make out the words past the ringing in his ears. He presumes from the tone the conversation is something along the lines of what the fuck are you two doing. Then a conversation above him at least peripherally as he lies crumpled on the sidewalk his arms wrapped around his aching ribs his lungs still searching for breath escapes him with the first assaults of the Tweedles.

The conversation carries on for a bit before the Tweedles issue a vague you'll be sorry to whoever it is has interrupted them and one last must be your lucky day to Jackie Boy as they dump his ass unceremoniously back to the pavement. They then walking back to their car and peeling off in a squeal of rubber and a blast of their police siren. Arms reach down and grab Jackie Boy by his shoulders to lean him in against the building and when Jackie turns his head and looks up he finds he's looking at an old cop buddy of his from back in the day as the expression goes.

Jackie, the man asks like he's uncertain he has the right name for what's in front of him, as he takes a step back away from Jackie Boy to reexamine the man and the situation to see if it jives with his memory of this experience.

Eddie Kennan is the man's name and Jackie hasn't seen him on forever and a day not since Ol' Jackie's little unauthorized trip to Biloxi back in a different age. Jackie's surprised to see him now and of all the chance encounters to have Jackie Boy thinks this one is nearer the portion of the list under the heading of quite possibly the least likely.

His ex-partner, Ol' Eddie Keenan had been called 'Fast' Eddie back in his college football days, two years at LSU til his knee got blown out and any hopes at the NFL were lost. Ol' Eddie Keenan had the smarts though to stay in school and get the all-important college degree before moving back to New Orleans taking the civil servant exam and becoming part of NOPD. His career unblemished and tacking a fast track to the top til he'd had the misfortune of Ol' Jackie Boy as his partner right before Jackie's spectacular, near legendary cash out from the force, the aforementioned Biloxi bad mess Jackie Boy had gone out on.

Jackie hadn't blamed Key for not standing by him for the colossal fuck up of his. He knew Key couldn't afford to do so for his career's sake which was still certainly stained anyway by association if nothing else. Still, the man bore no grudge against Jackie which spoke well of his character, just a silent, stoic shaking of his head over someone determined to destroy himself.

Key is looking Jackie Boy up and down apparently no less surprised at the encounter with Jackie as he helps him up from street where he'd been spending entirely too much time of late.

"Damn Jackie," he says once he realizes who he has here standing next to him, "would have thought you dead for sure by now. Hell, I'd have put money on it," Key says.

Key being the nickname he'd earned on the force and much preferred over the 'fast' Eddie moniker which he'd never much appreciated for the sordidness it implied.

Jackie Boy wants to say something clever in reply some smartass retort like, you should see the other guy or how the gods find him to amusing to let him be dead just yet but mostly Jackie's just trying to catch his breath. Key helps keep Jackie Boy upright against the wall with one hand's fingertips pressed into his shoulder as a counter balance against gravity.

"Still doing your hero routine aren't you Jackie Boy," Key asks him after a moments review from head to toe, Jackie seemingly living the phrase worse for wear though not giving it fair justice or accuracy. Jackie doesn't answer him as it seems more or less a rhetorical question than one already answered. Jackie straightens up and looks at his old partner in his off the rack non-descript suit a little thicker around the middle, a little more grey in his hair otherwise looking much like Jackie remembered him.

"Damn Key, but it's good to see you," Jackie says to him, "care to join me in a drink?"

"Fine Jackie," Key says after a moment's pause while he waits to see if Jackie'd remember Key gave up drinking a long time ago without holding out much hope of it happening.

"Don't tell me Jackie I don't want to know about anything your into or even near, and I don't want to be anywhere near when this misguided hero shit of yours"

Key looks like he's about ready to walk away from Jackie Boy but is wrestling with a debt or an obligation he feels to say something to Jackie. To call Jackie out on his need to pursue the misguided hero shit a refrain Key knows Jackie's heard about a million times before and never headed before and apparently hadn't given up at all judging by the situation Key had walked up on.

"Dammit Jackie," Key says and you can hear the tiredness in his tone, "don't you think you should give it up after all of this time?"

Key waits for Jackie to respond to the query, to see if there's some salvable portion of a rational sort somewhere in

Jackie Boy. Key doesn't know why he searches for this other than a grasp for one last shred of a hope or something like it. He should have known better after even his brief time with Jackie Boy, he simply didn't have it him.

"Nope not you huh Jackie," Key says when Jackie won't meet his gaze, "haven't learned a damn thing have you?"

Key shakes his head as he straightens up.

"Well I'll leave you to it then," and then Key simply walks away from Jackie Boy still being held up by the wall the last thing he says casually tossed over his shoulder after one step away is the admonishment for Jackie to watch his ass. Near always a piece of good advice though Key knows here it was going to go unheeded and unheard.

Jackie Boy doesn't begrudge Key walking away from him, it was simply a very smart move as Key himself has said, No use being anywhere near when the crashing comes. The specter of looming catastrophe which Jackie Boy seemed to specialize in, inviting it to visit his person somehow like an ancient hero sentenced to a colossal streak of bad luck in some form of punishment like handed down by the ancient Greek gods.

Part III: Ars Moriendi

The female of the species is more deadly than the male.

Rudyard Kipling 1911

Dirty Blonde

King's sitting in his office holding his pistol in his lap as he looks over at the pair of cops who'd been on his payroll since forever and a day. It was one of his first business transactions and one with a long history of paying dividends until the arrival of the hero on the scene. The pair presently in his office to deliver their bad news about the hero, old news as far as King was concerned the minute they showed up in his office sans one hero.

King's only half listening to their excuse for not having the hero between them as he ponders over what exactly he was paying this pair for if this was an example of their capabilities now. He's reassessing his relationship with the pair and wondering if maybe it isn't time for the termination of this relationship with these two. It was the secondary reason for the pistol in his lap as he felt threats all around him now in his weakened state and knowing this pair for being nothing if not opportunists and could not be considered to not be a threat to him.

The pair of tame cops are unapologetic as they stand in silence in front of King now as he mulls their story of having been thwarted once more in their efforts towards the hero. He's not pleased with this development but doesn't know what he should really have expected as everything else with this hero as gone sideways in some parlance so why not this as well. He thinks to harangue the pair or rant or rail against whatever powers which continue to intervene on the hero's behalf for whatever reason when there is the loud smack of a door thrown open behind the pair making them jump and throwing King off his thought process.

The interruption comes from the rude and unannounced entrance of one Lisha Danner into King's office. She is dressed still in black in defiance of the heat as she moves right up to the desk and past the two plainclothes cops seemingly without seeing them though King is well aware of their presence when she begins her harangue.

The pair watches as Lisha Danner moves in like a predator into King's office, stalking him as he sits behind his desk. They're blown away by both her beauty and her comportment even if she has breezed past them like a malevolent storm you're frightened of even by proximity and silently offer up a prayer of thanks to whoever's listening for it having bypassed your own person. Turns out she's come to confront King about the two of them in and odd twist of fate or coincidence would have it.

The gist of what is generously described as a conversation runs along the lines of who does King think he is to interfere with her vengeance and the other thread of hadn't she told him she had it under control. King for his part can only retort with how it is his city not hers despite any birthright she might claim or lineage to Joey Bones, a mistake King will pay for in short order.

Richards and Thompson, the two cops, are enjoying the show if not fully following it as they watch as King uncomfortably absorbing the vicious arguments she's issuing for its own merits right up until the moment King points them out to her. She, thankfully, only glances at them for the briefest of moments as they stand frozen trying not to look like any kind of a threat before she returns to King and offers up the following quick assessment of them.

"What these two morons" Lisha says pointing at and then looking over the pair of low ranking plains clothes vice cops.

"Please tell me you're kidding Lucien," she says as she's turning to look at King her momentum momentarily arrested by this farcical explanation of his. Thompson and Clay are momentarily stunned and well-nigh unpleased to have drawn her attention even for a moment however brief and stiffen up like corpses in an unpleasant comparison. They're relieved in fashions they don't properly understand when she returns her attention back to King.

"Fuck you Alicia," King says. "Asking me how I dare, who do I think I am?"

"This is my city Alicia or Lisha or whatever the fuck you wish to call yourself these days," King says literally spitting mad, "so who do fuck do you think you are?"

King in his anger has risen from his chair punctuating his points with the pistol near forgotten in his hands, its nose dancing along the tip and edge of the large desk. Alicia / Lisha takes a step back from King like distance can matter in a gunfight. She keeps one eye on the pair of dirty cops as she sinuously moves to put herself in a more advantageous position as she subtly reaches in to the small hand bag hanging at her waist near her hip for the little automatic she kept there.

King's still growling out sentences about this being his city, how Alicia should leave the hero and the city to him and other unflattering things about her interference with things which bear not repeating. His anger had King unfocused and distracted if still armed. Alicia was calculating her odds with the distractions and the addled state from the combined effects of King's pain and his medicinal use of whiskey pain and pain pills and liked her chances.

Alicia remains perfectly calm as she moves in the room to keep all three men in her line of sight. Lucien's pair of cops seem transfixed by her which gives her a little smile of satisfaction. She determines they're beings who are easily swayed as she watches them watch her and the way her hips move. She decides they won't make a decision preemptively which moves her attention back to king still grumbling his list of complaints about the situation presently and what not his attention focused elsewhere and not in the here and now.

Though its earlier than she'd planned for, here was an opportunity for her to exact the revenge she'd had planned all along for Lucien while he was distracted by his anger and not entirely lucid from it combined with the whiskey and pain pills. The gun in his hand can make it a case of self-defense should she need any explanation though she does take a look back at the cops and knows she won't have to worry about any need for this.

The beginning of a smile curls up at the corner of her lips at the early arrival of her timetable as she decides to embrace the no time like the present and her smile broadens as she turns to face the man called King.

"Haven't you heard Lucien," Alicia asks him, her pistol out but still in her hand and at her waist and not immediately visible.

"Hear what Alicia," King says agitation still in his voice his eyes turned to her but the gaze is uncertain and more importantly unfocused turning the odds more in her favor.

"The king is dead," she said over her wry smile as she makes one last check of the scene. King looks at her trying to understand what she's getting at the pistol in hand at her size no registering in his mind. He looks from her to the pair of cops who are of no help and then back to Alicia and is no closer to understanding what she's said, it's meaning or importance here.

"What in the hell are you talking about Alicia," he asks her, his tone filled with an undercurrent of doubt and confusion which cannot be hidden. His anger is still riding the surface of his person though and remains in control to his detriment at reading the situation here right up until the moment Alicia's pointing a stubby little pistol at King.

Somehow he feels like he really shouldn't be too terribly surprised to have her holding a gun pointed at him. He and Alicia, pardon Lisha Danner have been heading towards this moment since she arrived back in town and it still seems the appropriate conclusion for the pair if perhaps in an anticlimactic moment reached too soon. An irrelevant point too as King knows, whether she calls herself Alicia or Lisha Danner or anything else she hasn't changed so much for him no to well enough know she had every intention of shooting. Hell, she was probably already squeezing the trigger the damn dirty blonde.

King holds this though while waiting on her and then he decides in one last act of defiance to hurl a curse at her for the last words to leave her with ringing in her ears and shouts out his last thought to her, "You damnded dirty blonde!"

"Do shut up Lucien," Alicia says to King as she fires her pistol multiple times at him as he stands behind the desk like she'd learned from a former lover of hers. She's trying to make up in number of bullets for the relative low punching power of the round the little pocket automatic of hers fired.

King tumbles under the hail behind the desk and out of sight as the smoke from the gun sings Lisha's eyes and her ears registered some ringing even from her little pop gun as her ex-lover had always derogatorily referred to it. In his defense held also called it an excellent little gun for a little lady and here in this instance her use of it had proven him correct.

She has a little upturned smile at the corner of her lip shooting Lucien has proven more satisfying than she'd have though it might be. She'd been half expecting some sort of a letdown when the act of actual vengeance occurs like it could not live up to the hype and build up in her own head. It hadn't disappointed her. Hell she thinks the feeling of it is akin to great sex or at least it was similar enough such was the pleasure and fun she felt from the shooting and making the quip delivered a reality. She can only hope it's as good with the hero when his time comes.

She turns round to look at the pair of cops still standing there shocked at what has just occurred in front of them on so many levels with one layer of shock still to come. This second shock arrives shortly when the blonde woman whom they've yet to be introduced to, moves sinuously and sexily to slither in behind the desk oblivious or pretending really well about the body must be there at her feet.

She sits and calmly removes the clip from her gun before doing a quick rustle into her small bag before pulling out a second clip which she snicks in place before performing a coup de grace as her ex-lover had told her was both necessary and simply prudent to the body on the floor.

She brings the gun up even with the desk and casually points it at the pair as she looks them over. She's pleased to note how the pair of them are unable to keep their mouths from dropping open in a wow expression as Alicia just chuckles at their befuddlement without lowering the pistol aimed at them. She's trying to decide if these two are or can be useful or if she should shoot them too and be done with it.

"Well boys," she says to them her voice warm if a little scratched. It's the voice she uses when she wants to keep the man she's targeted off kilter and preoccupied by the idea he might actually see her naked or in his higher hopes, have sex with her like she presumes these two have already envisioned.

"The King is dead," she continues, "so the question now boys is join me or join him," and here she points down in the general direction of the still warm corpse at her feet. King's pair of bought cops still stand where she'd left them and are looking at her a moment longer mouths slightly still agape over the actions so recently committed and the change in temperament of the blonde before them through at least three phases including this new one before them now.

"Unless it's going to be a problem," she asks tired of waiting on them they then look at each other as they quickly sort through the decision making process together. The cops work their collective brain to do some quick and very dirty math while trying to ignore an underlying idea of sleeping with her too, to muddy up the works just as she'd already guessed.

Despite all of their other faults and despite her previous derogatory reference, they agree to align themselves with her by nodding their heads vigorously in the affirmative not trusting their mouths not to say something stupid to a woman holding a smoking hot gun. Lisha's pleased with this acquisition of assets and smiles a wicked little grin over the victory won.

"Say it out loud boys," she says as she sits back in the chair the gun still pointed in their general direction. She's debating putting her feet up on the desk top to give the boys a glimpse of her killer stilettos but decides not to when she has to stifle her own giggle over the imagery the phrase invoked realizing they really were killer heels now.

"Come on now boys," she says still smiling, "I need to hear it from you. I need to hear you say it out loud now boys. I don't have all night"

"Yes," they say in unison as there's no doubt in their brains about serving under Lisha Danner in any capacity. Lisha smiles as she sets her pistol down on the top of the desk and then rummages through Lucien's desk for a glass which she sets on the desk top and pours some of his whiskey into she raises it in a toast to herself says cheers boys to the cops before downing it in one go and pouring herself a second one which she intends to savor by drinking it slower.

She hadn't necessarily intended for this but she realizes from her seize the day moment she now sits on the edge of an opportunity here for her. She can inherit Lucien's empire and accept it as a new challenge for her. An unplanned way for her to do something new and make her own way in the world make her mark and again the wry smile cured up at the corners of her mouth at the timing of the idea.

Her runway quality wry smile plies her lips at the serendipity or confluence of this opportunity here. She'd been getting tired of New York anyway and though she hadn't been able to put her finger on it she realized now she'd been searching for a new avenue to take her life into.

She'd been feeling restless in her New York life anyway, knowing it was nearing its end as she'd dared to get older and had simultaneously refused both surgery and drugs to stay thin and facing judgment because of it. She had to admit to herself though she'd have never thought a return to her roots to avenge her brother Joey Bones would be road to take her towards the start of a new enterprise.

Lisha Danner nee Alicia Bonnamo was adjusting to the idea of it, trying it out the sound of it in her mind as she sipped the whiskey. She begins sketching out a preliminary outline of hat she'll need to do if she should choose to take the empire which is ripe for it. First the hero tough, she won't be distracted from it like king had let himself be and then after well, we'll see she thought to herself when the scene is interrupted by the new consigliere here as well when he walks in a moment later looking for King.

The man quickly assess the change in the command structure but makes the mistake of protesting too much and too loud for Lisha Danner's liking. She looks past the man at the pair of cops indicating this is a problem for them to solve for her thinking this is as good a place and as good a way to test their newly sworn allegiance to her person.

The cops don't disappoint her as they drag the consigliere from the room and out of sight. She rolls over the idea recently formed in her head. She had these cops on board and the King dead, so where does this leave her she smiles as she thinks of some movie. The King is Dead, so all hail Lisha Danner, the new queen of the city!

She so liked the sound of it.

Sixes

Jackie Boy sat a long while with no-one in any hurry to chase him away and no-one really paying attention to him either, left alone as he looked like a man who wanted this more than anything and he did even if he didn't know it. He's got spots of his own blood on his clothes and a large clot on the side of his head. He's also got last night's stench and dirt in his clothes and dried sweat underneath from his encounter with the Tweedles.

He's well aware how he's a sight now after his encounters and won't be able to stay here long before one of NOPD'S *cough* finest rousts his ass despite the still early hour. It was

one hell of a way to start a day though Jackie realizes he's
mostly still finishing off the night before to be technical about
these kinds of things. Either way though, he's still in too sorry
a state for public appearance even acuity known for being
forgiving of public excess which seems like it would be some
form of weird accomplishment or mark of pride in the long
history of the city of New Orleans.

He's sitting on a bench atop the levee watching the river
go by though still not far from Sissy's place if he can make it.
He's planning to do exactly this but first he simply needs a
moment, a small respite to gather him back together or a
reasonable facsimile of it before making the attempt. It's a
momentary piece of quiet he has here, a small respite in the
never ending trudge of what passes for his everyday life.

Jackie's feeling caught between forces he knows he
doesn't understand even slightly, tossed about like the Greek
heroes at the whims of beings with their own agendas and safe
in the knowledge how no one can call them out on their
actions or hold them accountable. Jackie being bounced about
casually and carelessly between the thin man and this new
blonde and the man called King and the ghost of Sissy even if
he hadn't seen her since that first night and assuming he had
then there as well. Jackie Boy well caught on the famous

thought from some damned novel, solidly in the middle of damnded if you do or don't and seemingly with no way out.

Jackie raises the tallboy to his lips and takes a long pull from it wondering how it is he manages keep getting himself solidly in the middle of stupid scenarios like the one he finds himself presently in. It was a singular talent of some form to retain this solid streak of bad luck of his which seemed to always manage to take even the most benign situation and spin it up into catastrophe.

Jackie'd always thought the whole notion of nothing to lose was supposed to give the hero strength or resolve or some form of indomitableness which won't allow him to loose. Some hidden reserve which would see him through to the end of things and through the terrible obstacles and terrifying enemies. The journey ending of course with the bad guys vanquished, the girl saved, and the hero injured and kissing her.

He was fairly far from this stupid heroic like notion. He'd gained no traction in his quest to save the girl first and no further ground now in the turn at avenging her. Between his own wide streak of bad luck and the assistance of the Tweedles and the distraction provided by the new blonde, Jackie had been drawn off course and deterred with nothing to show for and possibly nothing to come of it either.

He has not found the man called King and certainly has not avenged the girl lost. He has alienated himself from what he once knew specifically the mistress and secondarily his old place. He'd never had much but has gone from this a man living on borroweds. Borrowed time and a borrowed place which he should head off to and crash for the night.

He feels how it makes no damned difference either way he should choose or not choose. Hell, if he were feeling like pegging it a skosh more accurately he'd admit how he has had little effect throughout the narrative in the way things should fall. Made little damned difference or dent at all to alter the girl's fate except maybe as a catalyst of the harm which had befallen here.

Even any satisfaction in enacting revenge of any sort, which is so often a hero's raison d'être would only be a temporary victory and feeling more and more like a Pyrrhic one. Hell, Jackie Boy well knew how past a certain point it wouldn't even be remembered and one day it will all be over.

Luckily though, Jackie Boy remembers how he isn't any hero and this isn't any hero story being told here. The hero narrative doesn't suit him, or so he has been told repeatedly and most recently if memory serves. Why he felt the pressing need to attempt to continuously disprove this point was a mystery for the ages.

Jackie takes another sip of his tall boy and gets up to head back to Sissy's to hide away from the world for a little while.

Jackie lies down in the bed he and Sissy had once shared, he the interloper she the gracious host and only one of them realizing it was merely an interlude and nothing won which to build anything real or imagined. The sheets remain where they'd been left the morning a day or longer now, Jackie Boy unable to get an accurate telling of the time between the alcohol in his system and all which has transpired in the past number of hours. More things experienced than the time allotted would seem to allow for in a so many hours in the day way.

He lies down in the bed without bothering to change or remove any of his clothes. He takes a sip of his tallboy to help his body settle in to the pain which is only now registering from all points and provinces in his body back of his mind to fill it in on all of their complaints.

It seems a little late to come to this conclusion now, but somewhere Jackie Boy feels like he'd gone seriously off course. It's an unpleasant thought dredging up as it does so many different possibilities going back a lot farther than Jackie Boy cared to reflect upon. He'd never been the type to look backwards in any shape or form, a move forward kind and wasn't particularly appreciating the review now.

He snorts back a laugh as he takes another sip from his tall boy and swallows some aspirin held found in the medicine cabinet. He's laughing at the irony of the review, the promised flash before one's eyes of their life though this was more like a greatest hits album than a flashed review and he doesn't know if it it's arrived too early or too late.

He's wishing for sleep for some respite from all this troublesome thoughts and the very real aches and pains. He finds himself wishing for the pleasure of Sissy crawling into the bed to lie next to him, to feel the press of her tiny body against his and the offer of comfort and the promise of more.

Jackie falls into the space between actual restful sleep and fitfully tussling against falling too deeply into anything restful. This is a dangerous space as the mind is still free to wander without supervision and to dredge up a memory of Sissy and make it feel like a dream. It's a memory of a brief argument they'd had once when Jackie Boy had ignored her imploration to not tell her a certain phrase knowing it wasn't for them and still he had done this not hearing her or catching her meaning and seriousness.

He'd thought it appropriate for a tender moment they were sharing and he'd only whispered it but she had stiffened under his arm and then sat up in their bed and looked at him sternly in the darkness. Two mistakes actually one about love and the other about belonging to one another like it was an actual possibility.

"That's a lie Jackie." Sissy says rather vehemently, "I'm not yours and never have been. You never could get this straight in the damned thick head of yours!"

"We don't belong to one another Jackie," she exclaimed in a tone somewhere between rage and sorrow peppered in its undercurrents. "This is stolen time this interlude we share together but it's all it is, an interlude!"

Jackie mumbles something to here in disagreement. It's mostly inarticulate as he doesn't really have a strong counter argument to provide to her. It wouldn't matter if he could have found the words. She's having none of it as she sits up in the bed with her head down and the sheet held in front of her in a sudden interest in modesty or of a need for some form of protection however thin. She falters or pauses for a moment or perhaps simply pauses as she measures out the words she's about to dispense like a spoonful of unpleasant tasting medicine, pausing before delivering the hardest words which threaten to land in the harshest form on a person unaware of what's coming.

"Jackie," Sissy tells him after a sigh of defeat, "you can't give yourself to me or to anyone. You're already claimed. You already belong to someone whom your committed to much more than you could ever be with me or anyone else Jackie."

"You belong to the city Jackie and not to me at all," she says not looking at him, not wanting to see if the words strike or not. Fearful they'll strike to accurately or, and more likely, not dent his thick skull at all and everything be for naught leaving her with a decision to make.

"It's the city who you belong to, who you love and always has," she says sucking in a deep breath her back shuddering as she releases the deep breath.

"The city is your woman Jackie," she says, "she owns you and it is here to whom you're committed to. The city is why you can't give yourself to anyone and why we can never be because no woman can compete with the city."

Jackie Boy's about to say something anything but she's not finished and continues on before he can mount any defense or counter to her thoughts.

"It's not your fault Jackie," she says, "except you can't see it. You don't seem to know it but you love this city and she's your woman like no other woman can be strange and exotic and dangerous and leaving no room for anybody else Jackie."

"It's never me Jackie," she says stifling back a snuffle or a tear as she starts to rise up from the bed they were sharing a moment ago her nude back glowing in the light from the streetlamps, "and it never will be Jackie."

She stands up completely with the sheet dropping away allowing a glimpse of her perfect little ass as she steps over to the bathroom away from him creating some distance between them, and whether it's subconsciously or purposefully done is really unimportant as opposed to the very real space created as a symbolic rift between them turned into a physical reality.

Jackie doesn't have the chance to ask or catch her as she's already moving away from him. She steps to the bathroom and closes the door. After a moment Jackie Boy hears the shower turn as he wonders at what she's said and what he's to do with the information she's provided him while feeling that there's very little which can be done about it.

Her last steps away had carried a hint of finality to them, and Jackie Boy recognized this as the last moments for the pair of them no matter what he himself decided to do about it Her mind was made up and there was no going back.

Voodoo

Jackie Boy wakes from the dream spent and thirsty his clothes sweated through and lying cold and stale against his skin. He swears he can still feel the space next to him filled with the presence of the girl only just left and can feel where her body had only just recently clung to his own.

This isn't an accurate representation he knows, she doesn't cling and never has. She's not here nor staying as a ghost or a haunt or out of any sense of still belonging to him or this particular scope of the curve of time and feeling a need to cling to it like she's missing it or any part portion or kith and kin of it. She never had been about anything more than the moment and if Jackie Boy could remember correctly she'd placed little value in the things of this place when she'd been alive. If he could further recall he'd remember how she'd forsaken her family name and fortune and had instead chosen the life she's led without shame or worry about other's acceptance of it.

It's Jackie Boy who cannot let go of the memory which doesn't want to stay nor carry the burden of whatever the hell he's gotten himself into. No surprise really, the memory mimicking the girl as she was in real life. She's never wanted to be the reason for anything before, had never wanted the values or charter projections he'd tried to assign but he'd never heard her.

He'd told himself then he'd loved the girl for the weight of what those words were worth in comparison to the damages done because of the thought and the use of a word who's meaning Jackie doesn't really know. He hadn't listened to the girl when she'd told him nor the mistress either, making his way forward however mistakenly and despite plenty of warnings about his penchant for hero shit however misguided and misdirected and the girl paying the price for it, for his foolishness. So many lies told and most of them to himself and yet, here he still was right back in it just like the mistress had said about up to his head in it with more still to come knowing his luck.

Jackie Boy had lived all along thinking he could take anything life could do to a person and had. He hadn't ever stopped to consider whether there would be repercussions or what they might possibly be. Didn't understand there were long term effects from such a policy, effects which visit in a long overdue bill come to collect finally. Leaving the question begging to be asked about the value versus the price paid as if any part of it could be undone.

The girl was still dead and gone now like Jackie Boy needs a reminder how there's a price to be paid for daring things when the understandings of them are not clear with too many different definitions available to cloud the issue. He already carried the weight of her loss like a millstone, an unfamiliar guilt which was what was really clinging to him as opposed to a ghost or some other phantasm.

The memory of the girl which he cannot and probably should not forget as it had been the whole the catalyst or plot line for everything he'd done and had been done back in response to it. Some form of trade unconsciously agreed upon by both sides to engage in a doom loop each response met with an unequal reaction though a reaction all the same. Even now these things were playing out, the lost girl the cause behind the thin man returning Jackie Boy from the grave to avenge her when she'd never asked for anything from him.

The girl's dead and gone and he's still here and he wonders which one it is which is being punished. First he'd said he'd loved her and then he'd said he'd not forget her when this is possibly exactly what they both need. Jackie Boy has lived life too much without thinking on any future past the next few seconds or minutes so it's strange to him this promise and he doesn't know the trick of not forgetting the past without losing the present or dwelling on things gone and done.

The cliché says live for today and honor the past or some such. Right, sure. Like it's so damned easy a thing to do, so damn simple a task completed. Live and remember because here's a stone cold truth for you: she's dead and gone no matter which you choose to do but it won't change this central hard fact. Death is finality and there aren't too many arguments against this in any religion or science either. The one thing neither tells you, which no one tells anyone and which is the brunt of the burden is how hell is for the living and this is why they cling to the dead in selfish envious need.

Jackie Boy recalls how she'd said to let her go in her night visit, a gentle asking of him, and a prodding like a nudge to put him on the right tract. She'd asked this not so much for her but for him, for his own good and his inability to let her go despite it being the smartest path forward. Jackie's not certain he has the strength though to alter events despite knowing know how he cannot stay here at Sissy's place anymore if he ever really truly wants to fully escape from this loop he's caught in.

He's wondering if there's a point beyond entertainment or being sport for beings more powerful than he like the thin man clearly was and the physical strengths of crime lords and never mind new blondes who are sure to be the death of him. All this haunting from one blonde and predatory games from the other blonde, all Jackie Boy needs now is for the thin man to make an appearance to finish the day off. A phrase he regrets thinking the minute it appears in his brain.

Jackie leaves Sissy's place to go almost anywhere to grab a drink or a tall boy from whatever's open the closet to his location. He walks a short distance and finds a place still open at whatever dark hour this is. He doesn't wear a watch and hadn't checked the clock before he'd left Sissy's place, he just knows it's late by the dark tinged with a hint of light streaking in from the east do he presumed some hour just before the arrival of dawn.

He decides to head towards where the Cathedral sits sit in the park there facing the river and watch the sun rise and streak the sky for lack of anywhere else to go. He sits on tone of the posts lined along the street where the carriages will line up for the tourists later in the day sipping from his beverage watching the world go by even at this late hour.

Dead man, a voice says tight in his ear causing Jackie Boy to spin hard round almost dropping his beer in his haste to see who is standing there already knowing who to expect. There's no one standing there but he can still feel a chill on the back of his neck and he curses the stupidity of his shortsightedness for even thinking the thin man's name knowing you cannot be casually calling the devil's name and then dare to think he won't appear.

Jackie turns back round more slowly now to face the frightening form of the thin man before him.

"Straight fuck man," Jackie Boy says, "scared the shit out of me! Wear a bell or something!"

The thin man laughs his short laugh a slice of what Jackie boy presumes passes for a smile crosses his lips. He even tilts his head back like the laugh is an especially enjoyable one.

"Dead man," he continues, "Do you think it would do any good," he asks and Jackie Boy stares at him out of the corner of her is eye trying to make out the thin man from the dark. To separate the form from what clings to him in what appears to Jackie Boy to be an adoring, loving caress. Jackie Boy decides discretion is the better choice for him here and doesn't answer the question put to him. He takes a sip of his tallboy despite the buildup of foam at the top from its shaken encounter and waits for the thin man to get to whatever point he's here to make.

The thin man clicks his tongue and removes a toothpick from between his teeth and holds it in his fingers as he looks Jackie Boy up and down.

"I'm disappointed dean man," the thin man says to him, "the King is dead but not by your hand dead man."

The thin man leaves the statement there for Jackie Boy to contemplate and absorb. Jackie Boy's trying to decide if the man is lying or not, like it's some sort of a trick which would only seem appropriate for a man who the first time he'd encountered Jackie had thought of as the tall thin man.

"You didn't complete the job dead man and your girl lies unanswered for," the thin man says making an especially pointed point towards Jackie Boy.

"Unavenged you mean," Jackie Boy says and the thin man spreads his hands to indicate how it's a matter of definitions and whichever one suited Jackie was just fine with him. Semantics a fine point with the thin man normally but not in this instance. Jackie Boy wonders what this means for himself and the thin man, let's call it an arrangement, he has with the thin man. The whole raised from the grave thing let alone the piece of Jackie the thin man had appropriated and then returned to him. It had seemed a shitty deal for Jackie Boy but what else really should he have expected after all.

"So what now," Jackie Boy asks again with the damn laugh from the voodoo man which he now knows, understands *is* his name and the man's proper title if never to actually be used or said lest the man himself should come calling as Jackie had accidentally done this very evening. The thin man pauses for what feels a very long time which seems to stand still a picture rendered more acutely when Jackie Boy looks up around the two of them and the world looks to be standing stock still from the streets to the clouds. It's one of the most distressingly disturbing things Jackie boy had ever seen and he quickly focuses back on his tallboy as he waits on the thin man.

"Our deal is rescinded," the thin man says not looking at Jackie Boy who wonders at what this exactly means. He shifts in his stance hyper aware of the thin man and the power he projects, the scar on his chest begins to first itch and then ache. He briefly wonders if this is what a heart attack feels like as he clutches his chest before falling to the ground.

The thin man kneels down nest to Jackie Boy his wicked look black flame blade in his hand with a flick from out of thin air. Jackie knows what's coming next but it does nothing to alter the level of pain as the knife reopens the scar on Jackie Boy's chest followed by the digging around with his long fingers and pointed nails. The pain is excruciating bringing tears to Jackie Boy's eyes and a wish for a swifter death delivered.

The thin man licks his fingers and then sits next to Jackie Boy as he gently pats Jackie Boy on the should in what Jackie presumes the thin man thinks of as reassuring. The thin man sits down and seems far away like he's contemplating things.

"I let you live dead man," the thin man says after a moment his decision apparently reached. He stands up and nods his head after a quick review of the decision reached and seems about to step off away when a confused Jackie Boy stops him by stupidly asking the thin man why.

"Because death is too good for you," the thin man says and then laughs before he up and disappears back into the darkness.

Black Widow

Lisha Danner sits in her black bra and panties in front of a mirror carefully applying her makeup for the last act of her unfolding vengeance. She purses her lips to check her application of the very red lipstick and then sits back in the chair to turn her head briefly left and right to ensue she's achieved the effect desired.

She's going for the cliché of femme fatale, lifting a character from too many movies featuring the killer blonde but figures if she should pay homage then she should feature the whole gamut of the characterization. It's partly the reason for black in line with the choice to go blonde and now the last part, the applying of the very red lipstick to match the color on her recently manicured nails.

She approves of the visage before her and then she stands to step over to the desk where a black dress is ready for her to shimmy her way into complete with hose and heels, her killer heels to be precise followed by a smile at the reference made. It is her widow's black she dons though it is soon to be used in an alternate definition of the phrase.

She completes the look with her sunglasses and a small black handbag complete with her favorite accessory of late, the angry little pistol which has proven so adept at solving particularly irksome problems of late. With Lucien dead now, Lisha Danner nee Alicia Bonnamo has one last task to tend to. She smiles, a sly smile at the thought of one last assignation with the hero and the completion of her vengeance.

She pauses to make one last check of the mirror and then Lisha Danner heads out to meet the hero and bring her vengeance to a close. She smiles at a brief flit of feeling sorry for the poor dumb bastard knowing he doesn't see it coming, it quickly passes as she closes the door behind her and steps back out into the world.

Jackie Boy's sits on a bench not far from where he'd had his encounter with the thin man. It was about as far as he could make it considering the throbbing pain in his chest as he sits watching the world go by as he has no place to go so here is good enough. Hell, if he had something to put down in front of him he might catch some change from the passing tourists, mistaking Jackie Boy for one of the lost and homeless, though this isn't quite the stretch from the reality of things for Jackie as he thinks or would prefer to.

Jackie's pondering the questions of the universe as he sits there waiting for something which might move him or prod him in a direction. He's wondering what the thin man had meant about death being too good for him but thinks he knows the answer to the question. It hews in with what Jackie had thought previously about hell being for the living and this what the thin man meant when he left Jackie Boy to here to this life untethered and flying solo as it were.

The sun's moved to a higher position in the sky now as the day edges over into the early afternoon judging by the heat so common to the city and beating down relentlessly like it so often does past intermittent rain which only serves to make the heat more oppressive. Jackie's sweating rivers into his clothes which will have to be burned after he takes them off once he figures out where it is he can head to next without defaulting to wither Sissy's or The Mistress' which leaves him very few options past the shelter or the Y.

Jackie Boy's juggling random thoughts of a less perilous nature than the question the thin man had left him with, though this is only by a matter of degrees in comparison. He's thinking on blondes now knowing he cannot return to the one and feeling like he cannot get away from the other.

This new blonde haunting or hunting him for reasons unclear either way he wishes to phrase it. She confusing his memory of the lost girl and this one here presently, the past and the here and now freely intermixing in a confounding blend. Jackie Boy's chastising himself because he's been finding it hard to separate the two, to parse the difference.

Damn but this weight he was carrying was getting heavier. He didn't have a name for it but could feel it all the same. He's kicking himself for being distracted by and then from his sleeping with this other blonde, of getting lost in her sex as has befallen many a man prior but there's no comfort in the general numbers presumed in this statement.

It doesn't change how he feels it was a mistake made taking his focus and jagging him off track from the opportunity at revenge now lost with the death of the man called King, presuming of course the thin man had told the truth about this. An involuntary chill spikes up and down his spine at even daring to think this thought and Jackie Boy looks left and right for them man and is not afraid to utter a sigh of relief he hadn't appeared.

Worse is how he feels like he's betrayed Sissy somehow, even if it's just the memory of her, he still feels like he broke a promise though if he more accurately could or did recall he'd remember there never had been any promises between the two of them. She wouldn't allow it practically insisted on it like she knew better and he wonders if this blonde here does as well.

Lisha Danner, the blonde woman in question, the distraction providing him with a general feeling of all kinds of bad, a strange troubling of his conscience for once. A voice heard from a province long thought abandoned. The woman he was increasingly feeling like he shouldn't have had anything to do with despite the blur of blondeness she'd induced. Jackie Boy's kicking him for having allowed the blonde woman in despite his misgivings.

She'll be the death of him for certain Jackie Boy had said more than once without a touch of irony and not enough nuance in tone to convey the fright he feels behind this statement. He doesn't realize how prescient he was being all the times he'd been saying it like it wasn't some kind of a warning or at least a reminder to be mindful of these things. The dangers of bedding blondes one supposes.

There's a murmur which passes through the crowd from some point up the street which catches Jackie Boys attention and he watches as a ripple passes through the crowded streets and a part forms in the crowd though which he can see the blonde approaching. She's moving through the crows and homing in on him like a shark or missile or some other type predatory thing with only destruction bent on its mind. He watches as the crowd's part before her in fear or respect, he'll never know for certain but similar to how they had before.

She makes her way directly to him and where he sits. If he had the presence of mind, if there was still one possible shred of any kind of burst of speed or elusiveness anywhere in his body, he'd try to avoid her for certain. He'd try to duck or disappear. This is a lie he knows, feels she knows it too hence the confidence in the way she moves. He has no intent to miss her or possibly for her to miss him, because we're pretending for a moment how it's his choice here as opposed to a very definite lie told to himself his throat is dry as she comes up to stand before him.

She's dressed in her customary blacks once more in defiance of the heat or she oblivious to it, granted some form of immunity from the heat from places or beings which are best not thought to broadly upon. Jackie Boy watches her approach wondering if somehow she's heard him thinking about her and this is what has caused her to appear just like the thin man before in some kind of an eerier echo or some such appears because Jackie Boy was merely thinking about her. He's silently cursing his stupid ass for invoking her just like he had the thin man only so many hours before, a lesson unlearned despite its recent teachings.

Jackie Boy doesn't like the coincidence of this nor the comparison made between the thin man and the blonde as like creatures but he cannot dismiss it as a lark either. Considering his luck of late, okay his epic long streak of nothing but bad to worse, he thought it best really to see it as sinister and how it might actually warrant some wariness on his part. Jackie Boy thinks about his comparison her and self-consciously reaches to place his hand over the fresh again wound wondering at the damage she might do to him, is prepared to do to him.

This is all rendered moot when she drags her nails along a body part of his and produces much different chills than the thin man had. The chills make the promise he'd made to himself to distance himself from the blonde evaporate. They disappear like the warning he's only just held in the front of his brain yelling at him like the robot from a late 60's TV show; danger, danger! But he cannot hear it, and so cannot heed it.

"There you are," she says as she wraps her arms around his neck and leaning in to finish her destruction of his defenses with a kiss on his lips. It is no ordinary kiss either, but a kiss like she needs him and him alone, like his return of the kiss is the salve for the ache, the starvation she's felt in his absence.

She slithers her body against his ignoring the tackiness of his clothes no stale with both sweat and probable stink. She's softly saying things to him to prod him to movement so she can maneuver him to where she needs him to go. He hears himself agreeing to her suggestions, to the general idea of it despite his promise to defy her. He is swallowed under though by her spell of presence and perfume and promise of the tight clinging dress and what he remembers of what lies beneath it like so much sweet promise.

They go much like they had before on their previous encounter, stepping further into the strange surrealistic dream which is the two of them in this primal, animal attraction they share. He makes no note of this trip either, moments passing in a blur or he'd know she was taking him back towards Sissy's place, a place she shouldn't know about at all. They enter the house and stumble up the stairs and into the bedroom which awaits them.

She strips him out of his clothes and then guides him to the bathroom and into the shower reaching in to turn on the water and throw him under the spray. He finds a bar of soap handed to him and a kiss on his cheek before he's left alone. She unzips her dress and slowly begins to pull it away in a little striptease as she walks away to waits for him in the bed.

Jackie emerges still wet from the shower and joins her there as they work their bodies together in easy symmetry as he allows himself to get lost in her body and her sex despite all the warnings against doing the very thing. Hours or merely minutes pass and they finish this go round with each other and lie next to each other in silence as the sweat from their combined efforts settles and cools on their bodies tangled in the sheets.

They lie together for a time slipping in-between awake and asleep with Jackie Boy kicking himself for succumbing to the blonde once more without really understanding exactly how it had happened and in Sissy's place too. The second part was the more confusing as he had no idea how in the hell had they'd gotten here. He doesn't think he'd told this blonde about this place but then maybe he had and didn't recall a vexing question to go unsolved. There's always the possibility of it in the blur of blondes and the weight he feels for betraying Sissy in this way, and in her own true space.

Later in the dark as they lie apart and touching all the same, each with their own private thoughts as they drift in and out of sleep. Somewhere later in the dark Jackie in his half sleep stupor finds himself reaching for the woman next to him his only mistake is how he calls her Sissy when he finds her and tightens his hold on her. He feels her body next to him stiffen and become unwelcomingly rigid before she turns in the bed to escape his reach turning to sit straight up and hostile next to him in the bed.

She turns to face him holding the bundled sheet up to a line even with her collar bones to disguise her nudity. She grabs his shoulder with her hand blood red manicure perfect like her lips previously. Her nails though are sharp and digging into him to ensure she has his full attention. Jackie doesn't want to look at her though, feels it's something he dare not do lest he becomes lost in her, once a pleasant possibility and now one rife and fraught with all kinds of potentially bad things waiting to happen.

"Dammit Jackie," she says as she shifts her position in the bed to create some distance between them. Her anger has risen sudden and Jackie Boy doesn't quite know why as he's still caught half asleep as he struggles to rise to a level of consciousness which will allow him to at least defend himself but it's not an opportunity he'll find himself afforded.

"Stop calling me by her name Jackie," she says again putting on a serious pout while sending her anger towards him in waves across the bed. She's not really angry despite her acting. She's simply using the opportunity of the hero's utterance of what, Lisha assumes, is his lost girl's name like a gift for allowing her to make an issue of the name slipping from his lips as the reason for her being angry as too much of an opportunity not to be passed up.

Her anger over the use of the girl's name a ruse to allow her to storm off and go get her little pistol stashed in her little black purse hung with care on the chair by the bathroom during the otherwise careless discard of the rest of her clothes. She'd been waiting a good while for the opportunity to go and grab her angry little pistol so she could finally administer the final part of her revenge.

She takes his calling her by the other girl's name as an opportunity to pick an argument with which she can then escalate into a fight and all so she can get to the small bag hanging on a chair over there near the bathroom and her angry little pistol and shoot this sonnaofabitch and be done with it.

She almost feels sorry for the poor dumb bastard next to her who doesn't seem to suspect anything, doesn't know what's coming. Lisha knows how the dumb sonnaofabitch's about to be outmatched as she maneuvers the argument around the two of them and then back around until she's able to escalate it to the point where she can storm away in a snit.

She leaves him no room as she launches her anger against him. She lets him know how she doesn't appreciate the use of the other girl's name, how it makes her feel like she's an interloper, how she lies in someone else's rightful place. How it is patently unfair to make her compete against a phantom.

She insists he not call her by this other woman's name, to remember she's not this lost girl of his. She's rounding the corner and heading straight for the words which she thinks can cause him the most harm and still the poor dumb bastard doesn't see it.

She tells him this other girl's gone now, forever gone and there's nothing which can be done for her about it and Jackie's not helping her if he won't let her go. He can be here with Lisha now if he can let the girl go. Her last argument is a softer plea to free the girl and be with Lisha because the girl is dead and Lisha isn't and is tired of how Jackie keeps confusing the two of them, calling Lisha by the girl's name when she is not and cannot be her and it's not her name so please see her for who she is.

It's a good plea, but she couldn't prepare for or anticipate for the thickness of his skull and the shear impenetrableness of it. He mumbles something under his breath which she doesn't quite hear so she asks him to repeat it while expecting his customary return to silence as a reply.

"It wasn't hers either, not really," Jackie Boy inadvisably and unwisely repeats his original muffled thought, not her real name anyway.

Lisha's momentarily taken aback by his response and she pauses while she regroups, She'd expected him to be angry and to respond to her arguments accordingly, had expected almost anything other than this obtuseness from him assuming it's genuine, which she strongly suspects it is. No matter tough as she's quickly back on course towards the necessary dramatic moment she needs to enact the next step in her plan to complete her vengeance. She can still use this too to keep the hero uncertain and off balance until the last possible moment until she can shoot him.

"Really Jackie," she says incredulity dripping from her words and into her body language as she shifted her weight in the bed and began to rise letting the covers slip from her shoulders to expose her breasts but she's not self-conscious about the exposure. She never has been in all the time he's known her, which is a generous use of words to describe the amount of time spent and the depths reached of personal intimate knowledge.

"Is that supposed to be funny," she asks him not expecting or waiting for an answer as she continues to rise up from the bed. Jackie Boy suddenly realizes she's not playing, seeing her clearly for the first time no confusion as to which blonde she is but far too late to alter what he knows is coming next in their little play.

"Okay Jackie Boy," she says, "if that's the way you want to play it," she concludes, Jackie's able to feel the heat of her anger even at this distance as she storms away in a snit from their shared bed. She's outwardly angry keeping up the façade despite being inwardly pleased with her machinations.

She lets the sheet drop in one last tease as she walks away nude taking advantage of the fact she'd never been self-conscious. She's hoping this one last flash of her splendid little nude ass distractingly revealed in the intermittent moonlight and further scrambling the hero's thoughts as she leaves him behind her, no pun intended.

She briefly looks back over the room and the bed where she and the hero had lain but a few simple moments ago to check and fix the scene in her mind. She stops at her bag and grabs the angry little pistol before entering the bathroom to turn on the shower to drag the moment out a little longer, to allay any suspicions, She had another reason too as she sought and craved the anticipation of the joy and the pleasure she fully expected as she channeled her shooting of Lucien. She's hoping this execution will feel the same or better and a smile as she slips behind the door and begins to count to one hundred relishing the moment

She reaches the count she'd had in her mind and emerges from the bathroom to cast a sliver of light across the room to touch against the bed with the gun in her right hand. The steam from the bathroom swirls up around her as she waits a beat for him to turn in the bed so she might crack a smile, a single, simple little smile at the corner of her mouth to belie the entire joy which she fully intends to inhabit once her vengeance is complete.

She senses something's wrong though as she steps from the stream, it takes a moment but she realizes the hero's not in the bed. She does a quick look about the room and finds him standing, dressed and ready to leave apparently. He stands in front of the windows on the far side of the bed and Lisha Danner can make him out clearly in a soon to be fatal mistake made on his part. She smiles as she aims and fires at the hero without so much as a word said.

Lisha's shot at Jackie Boy punches him through the window and out to the small balcony ringing the house. His momentum doesn't stop until his side strikes the ubiquitous iron railing where he briefly catches his balance right in time for the second bullet to finish the punch and throw him over the rail to the street below. The only sign he's passed through is the curtains gently swaying in the open doorway.

Lisha moves over to the window and steps out onto the balcony to peer down to the street below. She sees the hero lying there crumpled in a widening pool of blood. She momentarily debates putting another shot into him but decides she doesn't want to break any further the previous stillness of this part of the Quarter at night.

Lisha looks down from the balcony and thinks to herself how between the bullet and the fall, this ought to do it for the hero. She returns inside and gets dressed in order to leave this place. She's in no particular hurry despite the efficiency and economy of how she moves. This is New Orleans after all, and it might be a while before the body is found even this early in the hour of day, in this part of the quarter. Still best not to be round when it inevitably is found, rather conspicuous lying in the street like it was.

She returns to the inside of the house and quickly gathers up her clothes getting dressed while also making sure she's not leaving anything of hers behind. A quick change into more comfortable clothes than the black's she's so recently been wearing. Her mourning was over despite the lack of having reached a year and a day as was usually dictated for in these situations. Neither Lisha Danner nor Alicia Bonnamo noted for any kind of streak of sentimentality nor a need to honor traditions possibly outdated.

A Southern Snow

Lisha exits the house and walks calmly over to where the body's lying in the street. She steps cautiously as she nears it squatting down to look at him for a moment, seeing him struggle for breath and his eyes no longer focused on this world. Satisfied he won't last much longer Lisha stands and then calmly walks away from the body in the street with the sounds of sirens still off in the distance.

She's traded her widow's black for a pair of tight blue jeans and a classic pair of Chuck Taylor's and a David Bowie tee. Her hair's slicked back and a cigarette newly lit dangles from her lips like the one from Bowie's visage on her shirt. She stuffs her sunglasses into the collar of the tee while adjusting the strap of the bag on her shoulder carrying what she's came into this scene with.

She heads off towards Canal and eventually back to Joey's place in the CBD where she plans to grab a long soak in the tub and a drink, and not necessarily in this order either. She's thinking as she walks away she thinks how she cannot wait to get her hair back to black a good wash and better dye job than the one to turn her to blonde. A professionally done now to hasten the return along an activity for tomorrow.

A small smile starts to turn up on the corner of her lips gradually expanding into a larger one as she delights in the idea of returning to her natural black and the opportunity to rest her life once more as she embarks on the new chapter. The idea of empire she's be entertaining since her successful resolution of the business with Lucien.

She thinks if this is to be a full reset then perhaps a name change is in order in keeping with her new identity. It had worked before when she'd gone to New York and become Lisha Danner but with the hero now dead she felt the name should be retired with him as well. She's reluctant to part with the name Lisha Danner as it had suited her so well and had augured a good era for her. The last use of the name Lisha

Danner had gone fairly well too and she smiles at the thought of its retirement. The next name she chooses for herself will have a legacy to live up to and must fit the criteria set forth her of serving her going forward it was something to think about as she soaked in the tub.

Lisha sits on Joey's couch wrapped in one of his shirts under her thick robe holding a glass of whiskey in her hands. Despite her lack of a belief in any version of the afterlife, she is also a child and citizen of the city of New Orleans which knows a thing or two about haunts so she silently offers up a prayer for Joey. It's a simple request for a speedy journey to whatever comes next after this life for her beloved.

Joey's the last man on her list to put to rest before she can complete here reset and become someone else and with the prayer said and completed when she raises her glass and lets a shot pour out from it before she throws and smashes the glass against the far wall. No more mourning or melancholia past staying in his place and keeping some things of his. More a reminder than a shrine, there's no need to be morbid about these things.

Lisha stands and moves over to the kitchen to grab another glass and some ice from the freezer. She moves to the counter and pours herself another drink. She raises it to her lips when the idea for her new name appears like magic in her brain. She rolls it over liking it more and more as she tries it out in her head before daring to say it out loud.

Sofia Snow, she says out loud softly at first and then louder the next time as she tests it out. She likes the alliteration of it and the incongruous imagery of it. The idea of snow this far south liking it for the mark of rarity it is and decides his name suits her and will be her new name will be for her new role in the world as the head of an empire.

She's still rolling and playing with her new name she's decided to adopt in her new role as she tries to get herself used to the sound of it. She moves back to sit on the couch with her drink as she worked to fit herself into the name Sofia Snow. Sofia Snow a name fit for a queen she thinks, Queen of the city or soon enough taking a page from Lucien and his ridiculous appellation. Well, she'd killed the King, Lucien, and still so very glad of it.

She was Joey Bonnamo's sole heir, and now, with Lucien's death she had the reigns and rights to an empire if not the keys. She'll take what's hers by her inheritance and step into her rightful place as queen of the city.

She has a lengthy to do list formulating in her mind starting with a call put in to her paired cops to let them know whose pulling their strings now. A gentle reminder to the pair as she plots out the first steps in the securing of her future empire. Some decisions are easy like how she's already decided she'll ever use Lucien's office, how she will use trusted proxies like the paired cops and other intermediaries to run the day to day of her empire. She thinks a different place all together on the very rare occasions she decides to grant an audience to anyone.

It's a lesson in plausible deniability to help keep her above and at least one step away from the real criminality of the empire to come. It's a thought process in which she'd been well schooled in by an Australian Special Ops soldier over one long summer they'd spent together. She'd been modeling in Australia and he'd been in-between assignments or some such. She hadn't cared to listen, but damn that man she nearly blushes at the recollection thinking she might have to give the man a call.

She has many decisions and miles to go before this comes to full fruition but it's something for her to work on tomorrow, tonight is for celebrating her vengeance completed. She raises her glass to her lips and takes a drink. She pauses for a moment to allow for a delightful thought to come completely forward as she walks to the windows of Joey's place, always Joey's place.

She raises the drink to the city outside and to her own reflection on this side of the glass. Her toast is simple as she notices her near gleeful smile: All hail Sofia Snow, the new queen of the city.

The Art of Dying

Jackie Boy watches her walk away from the bed admiring her ass as she does so and until she gently closes the bathroom door behind her after a brief pause at the chair and a gentle rustling of her things tacked there. When the door closes and he hears the shower start, Jackie Boy presumes he's been dismissed by her or this is an ending and takes the hint and the opportunity presented here to exercise the thought how now was perhaps a really damn good time to get dressed and then gone.

Jackie Boy thinking as he rises up to find his clothes scattered about on the floor how now was an excellent time for him to put a whole lot of got gone put between him and the blonde. He slides into his pants and throws on his shirt and is looking for his shoes when he realizes he's standing in a streak of light from the bathroom he looks up and over to see her standing there nude in the curl and caress of steam from the shower.

He's standing when she emerges from the bathroom with the pistol in her hand. She stands in the doorway naked except for the steam curling about her and surrounding her curvilicious form as she's framed and back lit in the bathroom door still slightly ajar. She's a vision standing there in the doorway rapped in nothing but the steam, Jackie Boy appreciating the imagery of a sexy naked woman fresh from the shower the steam curling round and caressing every part of her form.

Jackie's still appreciating the view and scanning his eyes down her body to take in more when he notices the gun she's holding. Intent to kill is plainly evident from the gun in her hand even if the reason is not, and a moot point with her intent plain and the gum already aimed. He barely has time to curse himself for the delay in realizing how it had been time for him to get gone, a realization which has come much too late to be of any use to him now.

He really shouldn't have been surprised to see her standing here like this considering he'd already admitted to himself how he'd thought she'd be the death of him. How he hated to be prescient if only in a past tense kind of a way as it were. He has a brief moment as he waits for the shot to ring out where he's trying to identify the point where it all swerved so wrong as if there was a singular point which could be named such and knowing the folly of trying to single one moment out when it was the story of his life. He's silently replaying the course of the past few days when the shot comes for him.

The first shot catches him about the shoulder and stands him up while knocking him a step backwards. The second and third strike him off balance and further backward to send him crashing through the window out to and then over the balcony to fall out to the hard street below. He hit's the pavement below in the shape of his own little crooked x marks the spot in some form of cruel irony or a mishandled channeling of dèjà vu.

Jackie's looking up at the sky as he silently counts all of his aches and pains. His one arm is smashed and useless next to his head and the other across his most likely broken ribs making breathing hard and raspy. He keeps loosing count he has so many and from the effects of the fade which has him in a permanent grip and getting stronger in near perfect reverse proportion to the weakening beat of his heart as it pumps out his life's blood through the wound delivered by the blonde who he no long. There was no confusing her with Sissy now in the twist of irony which is always cruelest.

While Jackie Boy lies there in the street waiting for death to finally at last come for him he's thinking about his streak of bad luck come to this conclusion. The punch line to the great cosmic joke, the long sick joke being played on him and running as a theme through his life with the difference this time being he was the only one claimed by it.

Jackie swears he sees a shadow moving up above him and looks up towards its source expecting he doesn't know what and sees the blonde framed nude in the shadow of the window. He swears she's still holding a smoking gun and a wicked if very pleased smile upon her face as she's looking down at what she has wrought and finding it satisfyingly concluded before she steps back inside and out of his view.

Jackie turns his head back to the sky to escape her gloating over his body as the last image which he's likely to see in this world. He can feel his heart slowing and the grip of the fade as it takes more and more of him, he feels a fog enter his brain and imagines he can see a short line of his, we'll call it mourners, the courtesy of not saying anything ill of the dead.

Jackie wonders who it is who've come to see the dead and for what reason, surprised to have any in attendance considering his record. The images comes into sharp focus for a second and he swears he can see the Mistress standing there alone at first until shadow joins herm a shadow in the form of the thin man. They both stand at the grave in one of the smaller cemeteries which are scattered about the city of New Orleans. No family plot for Jackie Boy and no paupers grave either, if they still have those things. And who paid for it he'll never know.

Jackie's not surprised to see how they both seem to know one another. Professionally they'd both tell you if asked. Sensible people don't ask though, discretion and valor kind of a sensibility from the files of if you know what's good for you kind.

Jackie imagines they've come to make sure death has really taken this time. The pair looks at one another, they nod their heads in silent agreement, a brief smile cracks the thin man's face and he offers his arm to the Mistress who takes it and is escorted away by the thin man as they continue their amiable chat.

Jackie Boy is returned to his battered and bruised body which is still lying in the middle of the street but with little time left. The last gift of dying is in knowing how close it is and Jackie accepting the time.

Jackie begins his shuffle off the mortal coil wondering if the devil knows he's dead this time.

AUTHOR'S NOTES

Memento Mori – Latin - Remember You Have to Die, 2ND DEF. An object serving as a warning or reminder of death, like a skull for example

Ars Moriendi - Latin - The Art of Dying

New Orleans is the setting and a character in this story.
No effort to accuracy was attempted in measuring distance, direction, or time.

All faults are intentional and strictly the author's who thinks he's being clever.

ABOUT THE AUTHOR

Jack Kelly is a pseudonym.

He has previously written about
Ol' Jackie Boy
In the story **"On The Bright Side."**

He has three more stories also set in the City Of
New Orleans with a very different
protagonist from Jack.
To read about the Haunt that Rocks The Crescent,
please read:

WAKE THE DEAD
RISE A HAUNT
THE TERRIBLE FRIGHT

All books are available at Amazon.com and Kindle